Praise for *The Boy, the*

"Weighty themes like courage, love, will, and care for the defenseless haunt this archetypal journey. . . . It is character development that shines most clearly, though the external environmental dangers and the mystery keep the suspense taut. . . . A poignant story."
—*School Library Journal*

"This first novel from Clark offers unusual imaginative and emotion-driven introspection, earning its several allusions to *The Little Prince*." —*BCCB*

"The creepy, atmospheric island gives the boy space to work through heavy issues, such as abandonment, death, and toxic masculinity . . . if readers are brave, like the boy, they will gain strength and insight from their time on the island. An unforgettable, life-affirming tale."
—*Booklist*

"In this touching debut . . . Clark writes with a lyrical and appealing rhythm, as she viscerally explores childhood emotions of fear and anxiety relating to bullying, abandonment, and getting lost." —*Publishers Weekly*

"[The boy]'s struggle to overcome his life-threatening fears illuminate how difficult it is to navigate the seas of growing up. His victory is a victory for all of us."
—Kathi Appelt, Newbery Honor-Winning author of *The Underneath*

"[A] well-crafted mystery-thriller . . . [that] speaks to the deepest level of heart and psyche, about facing the worst that fear has to offer, about determination and force of will, and about how the threads of love joining families together refuse to fray."
—Susan Vaught, Edgar Award–Winning author of *Footer Davis Probably is Crazy*

"Lyrical and hauntingly beautiful, this is a story for everyone who's had to learn to face their fears." —Jennifer A. Nielsen, author of *The False Prince*

"This mysterious gem of a book offers us solace and safety, without one note of false hope. Masterful storytelling."—Bethany Hegedus, author of *Grandfather Gandhi*

"Lyrical and evocative. . . . Several unexpected twists during a heart-stopping final act cap Clark's fine debut." —Janet Fox, author of *The Charmed Children of Rookskill Castle*

"*The Boy, the Boat, and the Beast* is an enchanting exploration of the power that resides in the stories we tell ourselves, and how we can change those stories . . . and possibly our own destinies. Heart-wrenching and hope-filled." —Nikki Loftin, author of *Wish Girl*

"Lyrical and heart-catching, *The Boy, the Boat, and the Beast* is also a page-turner of a mystery with a profoundly satisfying conclusion."
—Katherine Catmull, author of *The Radiant Road*

The
BOY,
the
BOAT,
and the
BEAST

Samantha M. Clark

A Paula Wiseman Book
SIMON & SCHUSTER BOOKS FOR YOUNG READERS
New York London Toronto Sydney New Delhi

SIMON & SCHUSTER BOOKS FOR YOUNG READERS
An imprint of Simon & Schuster Children's Publishing Division
1230 Avenue of the Americas, New York, New York 10020
This book is a work of fiction. Any references to historical events,
real people, or real places are used fictitiously. Other names, characters, places,
and events are products of the author's imagination, and any resemblance to actual
events or places or persons, living or dead, is entirely coincidental.
Text copyright © 2018 by Samantha Clark
Illustrations copyright © 2018 by Justin Hernandez
All rights reserved, including the right of reproduction in whole or in part in any form.
SIMON & SCHUSTER BOOKS FOR YOUNG READERS is a trademark of Simon & Schuster, Inc.
For information about special discounts for bulk purchases, please contact Simon & Schuster
Special Sales at 1-866-506-1949 or business@simonandschuster.com.
The Simon & Schuster Speakers Bureau can bring authors to your live event.
For more information or to book an event, contact the Simon & Schuster Speakers Bureau
at 1-866-248-3049 or visit our website at www.simonspeakers.com.
Also available in a Simon & Schuster Books for Young Readers hardcover edition
Book design by Laurent Linn
The text for this book was set in Adobe Garamond Pro.
The illustrations for this book were rendered digitally.
Manufactured in the United States of America
First Simon & Schuster Books for Young Readers paperback edition June 2019
2 4 6 8 10 9 7 5 3 1
The Library of Congress has cataloged the hardcover edition as follows:
Names: Clark, Samantha M., author.
Title: The boy, the boat, & the beast / Samantha M. Clark.
Other titles: Boy, the boat, and the beast
Description: First edition. | New York : Simon & Schuster Books for Young
Readers, [2018] | A Paula Wiseman Book. | Summary: "A boy wakes up on a mysterious beach with
no memory of how he got there and embarks on a journey to find answers"—Provided by publisher.
Identifiers: LCCN 2017045583| ISBN 9781534412552 (hc) | 9781534412569 (pbk)
ISBN 9781534412576 (ebook)
Subjects: | CYAC: Survival—Fiction. | Fear—Fiction. | Near-death experiences—Fiction. |
BISAC: JUVENILE FICTION / Action & Adventure / Survival Stories. | JUVENILE FICTION /
Social Issues / Death & Dying.
Classification: LCC PZ7.1.C579 Bo 2018 | DDC [Fic]—dc23
LC record available at https://lccn.loc.gov/2017045583

For my parents,
Paul and Fay Anne,
who taught me to love stories,

and to my husband,
Jamie, who always believed
I could tell them

A scream. A gasp. Then silence.

Flashes of light upon depths of dark.

The boy was small. So small.

Tumbled in the waves, tugged by the current,

round and round until the thin tide lifted him onto land.

I could guess how his story would end.

Fear destroys life. Eats souls.

And when fear is the obstacle, there is only one outcome.

I'd have to collect him soon.

I watched and I waited.

BORN

HIS JAW WAS THE FIRST THING TO MOVE, back and forth like a seesaw. His teeth rubbed against one another, pushing out the grit between them.

"Unhhh!" The boy's mouth crinkled.

He tried to open his eyes, but light slapped them shut again.

He felt cold, his back damp. He curled his fingers and was surprised they obeyed. He wriggled his toes, and they wriggled back. He lifted his arms, then felt around his body. Two legs, chest, head, and nose.

Just as it should be.

He pushed up on his elbow, and a sickening feeling erupted in his stomach. Leaning over, he retched, but nothing came.

I don't feel good. The thought slopped out of his murky mind.

The boy reached down to steady himself and a streak of pain ran up his arm. "Ow." He pulled it back, glaring at it through squinting eyes. There was no sign of injury. No cuts, or bruises, or scrapes. He pressed down again, but the pain bit back, clamping into his muscle.

"Ow!" His arm must be hurt on the inside, but how? *Better not press on it anymore.*

His head was sore too—a throbbing pain on one side. His fingers searched for the reason but found only curls of hair.

Struggling to his knees, the boy cautiously pried his eyes fully open, spying on his surroundings through gaps between his fingers.

He was on a beach of golden sand stretched out against the edge of a never-ending blue ocean. Curious waves crept up to him, then retreated, returning seconds later. The beach was cut off to his right by trees so large they hung over the water. Those trees fed into bushes behind him, then more trees and more bushes—a green wall, so thick he couldn't see through it, carving around the sand as it ran alongside the ocean into the distance to the boy's left.

That was it. That was all he could see.

The boy dropped his hands, the brightness no longer stabbing his eyes.

Where am I?

The question echoed in his brain and was joined by another.

How did I get here?

He gazed down at his body. He was wearing navy-blue swim shorts and a yellow T-shirt with a pattern on it. Nothing else. Not even shoes. He pulled at the bottom of the shirt so it stretched out before him. Even upside down, he could read the words: IN REAL LIFE I'M A PIRATE. The word "pirate" was curved around a picture of a skull and crossbones.

Skull and crossbones?

The biggest question of all screamed in his mind.

Who am I?

The boy staggered to stand. He was wobbly but stayed upright.

Had he just been born? No, he wouldn't be wearing shorts and a T-shirt if he had just been born. He wouldn't even know what shorts and a T-shirt *were*, or the beach, or trees, or the ocean.

He glanced at the emptiness around him. No ships or boats. Just rolling, white-tipped waves. The sand was clear too. No footsteps showing a path he had walked.

"Hello?" The boy flinched at the sound of his own voice. It was high and croaky, like a tiny frog. He coughed and pinpricks of sand scratched his throat. He stuck his fingers into his mouth and tried to fish them out, but they found nothing. His tongue was no help either.

"Hello?" he called, a bit louder than before. This time his voice was high, but singed with a rasp, like the words had been grated over the sand.

Still no answer came. The water's edge crept toward him, then backed away. The leaves in the trees purred in the slight breeze.

The boy's jaw tightened. He couldn't be alone. Not *completely* alone. There must be someone near, someone who could hear him.

He dug his feet into the sand, bent his legs as a brace, then gathered his voice from deep within himself.

"HEEEEELLLLLLLOOOOOO!"

An explosion came from the depths of the trees. A roar drove over him as every leaf and branch erupted. Riding atop the sound were the high-pitched squawks of thousands of birds, upset that their quiet had been disturbed. They rose up from the tops of the trees, so many that they changed the color of the sky. Circling above him, squawking in frightened, angry bursts.

The boy raised his arms to shield his head. Fear sparked in his belly.

The birds flapped their wings harder. Bones creaked as

they stretched with every beat. Their feathers stiffened to sharp, clanging points. The beaks lengthened too, gnashing with loud *clack, clack, clack*s. The noise grew deafening as the distended birds blocked out the sun.

The boy ran.

But there was nowhere to hide.

He scrambled across the sand away from the birds. But the ground trembled before him. Black spikes of rock shot up in his path, threatening to spear the boy.

Gasping, he turned back, but the birds still swarmed the sky above. The boy ran to the Green Wall. Dark, spooky, but maybe a place to hide. But when he got close, branches twisted and curled, creaking toward him. A loud *HIIIIIISSSSSSSSS* escaped through the leaves.

The boy cried out, then ran back and back as fast as his feet would take him. He ran until he splashed into the searching fingers of the incoming tide. The water had seemed calm before, but now greedy waves tugged at his ankles.

They wanted him to go in.

They wanted to take him down.

They wanted to drag him beneath

the surface. . . .

The boy fled to the center of the beach, the place where

he'd been born. He curled up as small as he could and shut his eyes tight. Everything had turned scary. Everything had turned bad. How was that possible?

"Once upon a time . . . ," he murmured. "Once upon a time, there was a boy who was hidden."

He waited for the birds or rocks or trees or water to attack. He waited to be hurt.

But nothing happened. After a while his heart slowed and the roar around him began to hush. The boy cracked one eye open. The birds had shrunk back to their normal size and jetted away behind the Green Wall. The trees swayed quietly in the breeze, their branches pointing to the sky. The sand stretched out along the coast, a pale ribbon that looked as soft as cream. And the ocean waves danced all the way to the horizon.

Quiet fell once again.

The boy's arms slid shaking to his sides.

He didn't know who he was or where he was, but he knew he wasn't safe on this beach.

And he had nowhere to go.

COMPANY

THE SUN SQUATTED IN THE SKY, WATCHING THE boy. He tried to return its gaze—maybe it knew a way out of this place—but the brightness hurt his eyes.

He stared at his bare knees, bare shins, bare feet. Skinny legs and arms like on a stick figure. He spread out his hands. Even with his fingers stretched as far apart as they could go, they were still small.

This didn't make sense. Boys weren't supposed to be left alone on scary beaches, were they?

Maybe there was a clue *on* him. He patted his pockets and felt nothing but dug his fingers inside to be sure. There was something. Something soft. He pulled it out and held it up.

A small piece of fabric, about three inches square, with fraying edges. It was bluish gray in color, although it looked stained and worn. And it had some fading markings, but the boy couldn't tell what they were.

He sighed. The square didn't have any answers. He stuffed it back in his pocket.

The label on his shorts was too faded to tell him anything, so he pulled off his T-shirt. This label had the words
DUDE DUDS and YM 10–12. The boy scrunched up
his nose. He felt sure he had a name but hoped it wasn't
"Dude Duds." 10–12 might be his age, though. His stomach tingled, like it knew he was right.

He pulled his shirt back over his head and looked
for more clues around the beach, anything he might've
missed. But there was nothing. Just the yellowish-white
sand, which looked as though it had once been bright
white but needed a good wash; the wall of trees covered in
every sort of green, from very light near the edge, where
the sun lit up the leaves, to an ominous black-green deep
within the branches; and the wide-open ocean that was
a thousand different shades of blue, swaying together as
though hearing the same silent music.

The beach looked harmless now. But the boy knew different. It was a trickster that was trapping him.

He wouldn't be fooled, though. He held on to one
hope, one small idea that simmered in his heart—he didn't
belong here. He couldn't remember where he'd got his
clothes, but he couldn't have gotten them on this empty
beach. This was the home of the terrible growing birds and
who knew what else. He'd heard that *HIISSSS* and he'd

felt the ground shake. Something else was in the Green Wall too. Something even more terrifying. He could see it in his mind—a beast like a giant bear with the head of a wolf, teeth sharp enough to tear apart a tree and a mouth big enough to devour a small boy.

The boy shivered. Yes, this was their home. Not his. He must have a different home, filled with clothes and toys and food and . . .

His stomach grumbled at the thought of food, and the boy sat up straighter. He hadn't eaten since he'd woken up, and boys were supposed to eat and drink, weren't they? He hadn't wanted anything before, but he had been busy trying to figure out where he was. Now that he thought of food, a craving crashed over him, racing from his toes to his mouth.

He pushed himself up to his feet. "I'll eat," he told himself. "After that, I'll be able to remember where my home is." But where would he get food? His brain gave him the answer: a refrigerator.

The boy's eyes widened as a blast of cold mist rushed at his face, stifling his breath. When the frozen air cleared, a large open box stood in front of him, illuminating shelves covered with food: a turkey sandwich wrapped in plastic; a half-eaten bowl of Jell-O; bottles of ketchup, mustard, mayonnaise; a pizza box; bags of broccoli and spinach; and, in a glass case, a cake with strawberry icing. On each side of him were open doors stacked with more shelves that offered milk, juice, Cadbury Fruit & Nut bars, cheese, and butter.

Everything looked delicious and the boy wanted to devour it all, except the vegetables. "Yuck!" But how could he? Was it real?

He touched the bowls and bottles. They were solid.

"How did this get here?"

He reached for a Cadbury bar first, but when he grazed the door's shelf, something white fluttered at the edge of his sight—something on the other side of the door. Was it more food? A clue? Vowing to eat the chocolate and cake as soon as he'd finished investigating, the boy pulled the doors shut.

The brushed silver on the outside of the refrigerator reflected his darker outline, and he stroked the spot where his face would be. He wished he could see himself properly, but the image was too blurry.

His reflection was broken up by other things: a palm tree magnet with the words MY HEART WAS LOST IN THE BRITISH VIRGIN ISLANDS, a magnetized clip holding a card for Great Smiles Dentistry with *1/9 2:15 p.m.* scrawled on it, a magnetic zombie with its arms and legs floating around its body, and in the middle, four shiny round magnets holding up the corners of a drawing of a knight on a horse outside a big castle. The knight had a blue cape flowing from his shoulders, and he pointed a long sword up to the sky.

"What's this?"

A tightness in the boy's chest made him think they were familiar, but he couldn't be sure. He liked the picture of the knight, though. He looked strong and powerful, confident that he could win any battle he faced. The boy plucked the picture off the refrigerator, his fingertips outlining the shape of the knight's helmet and sword. Smiling, he reached for the handle of the door, ready to eat, but his fingers clasped around air. His smile melted.

The refrigerator and picture had disappeared, and the boy wasn't sure what he missed more—the food or the knight.

A grumble echoed in his belly, and he muttered, "I know. I know." He pressed on his stomach to shut off its complaining.

Where did the fridge come from? Was it magic? He shook his head. That was silly. Magic was only in stories. Maybe he'd remembered it and imagined that it was here. Yes, that must be it. Just a memory that somehow came to life for a few seconds—a memory that wanted to tease him.

But if the refrigerator was a memory, then it must've come from his home, his real home. The boy's heart lifted. He was right, he did have a home somewhere else.

If he could only find it.

He collapsed into a pile on the sand. Nerves stabbed at his fingers and toes as he thought about what searching for his home would mean. The beach looked normal now, but he remembered how the rocks had tried to pierce him when he ran away from the birds. How the Green Wall had reached for him when he got close. How the water had tugged, tugged, tugged at him to go in. He'd have to leave the beach if he was going to find his home, but how could he?

"Once upon a time, there was a boy who was lost." The words crawled over the boy's lips, slipping past his despair. "The brave king of the land sent out a thousand knights to search every corner of the world. They searched the cities and the forests, the oceans and the beaches. Until they saw him, all alone. And they took him home."

He pressed his mouth into a thin line, an almost-smile grasping at hope. Yes, that was it. Someone would find him. Like the knight in the picture, someone brave and strong who could help him get home. He just had to wait.

"Chicken."

The boy jumped up. Whirled around.

"Who said that?" His voice was timid. He scanned the coast and peered into the thick trees.

Nothing.

Nobody.

He frowned. Had he imagined it? He dropped back onto his butt, digging his toes in the sand.

"You're not going anywhere."

The boy jumped up again. "Who said that?" He turned in every direction, strained his neck to see as far away as possible. But the voice wasn't coming from far away—it was right next to his ear.

"You're too chicken to find your way home."

The voice was so close, it could probably hear the boy's pounding heart. He tried to slow it.

"Who . . . said . . . that?" The boy eyed the shadows of the trees. Maybe the voice was from the terrible birds, hiding behind a thick trunk. If a shadow moved, the boy could run.

"I did."

A brisk breeze blew up and branches rattled. A bird flew out, but it was small and darted away.

The boy crouched down and felt for a stone or something to throw. But his fingers found only sand. He filled his fist with the grains.

"Come out," he said, trying to keep his voice calm. "Come OUT!" He threw the sand into the Green Wall. The grains fell through the branches—*tink, tink, tink*— onto the ground.

Nothing came. Nothing moved.

Leaves rattled in the wind. Clouds darkened overhead.

"If you're looking for me, you're way off."

Was it coming from behind him? The boy twisted on his heel.

"Where are you?" His hands thumped his sides.

"Here."

"Where?"

"I'm in here."

"In where?"

"In here."

His breath faltered.

"You're in . . . in my *head*?"

"Bingo. Gold star for the slowpoke."

The boy gritted his teeth. The air calmed and the sun came back out, but it didn't brighten his mood. He dropped onto the sand.

"What are you doing in my head?"

"Whatever I want."

"How did you get in there?"

"The usual way."

The boy crossed his arms. The voice was a bully that wasn't playing fair.

"Tell me how you know I won't get home."

"You're a scaredy-cat."

"No, I'm not."

"Yes, you are. I know you, and you won't leave this beach."

"You don't know me. You just got here."

The voice laughed. *"I'm always here."*

Pouting, the boy tried to remember the voice from before, but he couldn't. He shook his head. If he couldn't even remember his own home, it wasn't a surprise that he couldn't remember a voice in his head. Maybe the voice was right, even if it was a bully.

But if the bully knew him . . .

"Who am I then?"

"I'm not telling."

"Why not?"

"That wouldn't be any fun."

The boy narrowed his eyes. "If you're in my head, then you don't know anything more than I do, do you?"

"*That's for me to know and you to find out.*"

"Then what good are you?"

"*Ha-ha.*" The bully's voice sounded sinister. "*I'm no good at all.*"

The boy groaned and flopped onto his back. His only company was a voice in his head—and it was mean.

RESCUE

THE SUN RACED THE CLOUDS ACROSS THE sky, and too quickly it was heading toward the horizon. But the boy remained on the beach.

"Still think some knight's out looking for you?"

"Someone will come. You'll see."

He hoped he was right. The sun would soon leave him. And if he hadn't been found by then, he'd be alone. In the dark. Where any monster could see.

He glanced at the Green Wall. Light twinkled like eyes in the brush. Perhaps it was the birds, terrible or small. Perhaps it was the hissing thing. Or perhaps it was the other monster the boy knew hid behind the leaves, the half bear, half wolf that waited to eat him.

The ocean had swelled too. Rolling waves paced off the coast like they were searching for the right moment to strike. The moment when they could drag the boy down to the biggest monster of all . . .

watching . . .

waiting . . .

patient.

As the sun crept lower, the boy looked out for his rescue. But the beach held nothing except sand and rocks, sand and rocks.

Until he saw it. Something else, something new. Something small and gray bobbed up and down at the edge of the water.

He couldn't make out what it was. A hurt animal, maybe? It *was* moving. Sometimes it was short and fat, like it was trying to hide; then it would be hit by a wave and stretch long and skinny, as though it was reaching for the sand, reaching for safety.

The boy stepped closer, but not too close. Maybe the monster under the sea was trying to seize the gray thing too. His stomach twisted—for him and the thing.

"Stay with me." Words filled the air around the boy, and the pain in his head suddenly pulsed white hot. He clasped it with his hands as he whirled to see who spoke, but he couldn't spy another person. This voice wasn't the bully in his head. It was older, softer. *A woman.* It had felt warm and familiar, and the boy wanted to catch it and hold it close.

"Hello?" he called.

But the voice didn't respond. Had it come from the thing in the water? The boy peered closer.

"Don't go." The woman's words returned, dancing around him. "Stay with me."

"Who are you?"

Again no answer came, and no one else was on the beach. Except the gray thing.

The pain in his head dissipated, and the boy straightened. "Did you say that?" he called out, but the thing didn't reply, just shifted and curled in the tide. Maybe the voice had wanted him to help.

"You can't help that thing." Laughter tinged the bully's words.

"I might."

"The water will get you."

The boy gulped. The bully had a point, but if the gray thing needed his help, he couldn't ignore it. It was small; it needed protection.

Those words grew up from deep within his bones. Familiar and strong. *The smaller something is, the more it needs protection.*

How did he know that?

He couldn't say, but he knew he had to protect the gray thing before the monster in the sea ate it. If he was quick, ran lightning fast, maybe he could rescue it without getting pulled below. "I have to try."

The boy stepped closer, keeping his toes away from the greedy ocean. The gray thing drifted onto the edge of the sand, then was pulled back out again. In. Out. In. Out. Each time, it reached a little farther inland, then was sucked back out to sea.

"Let it go!" the boy shouted. "It doesn't want to be with you. It wants to be here with *me*. Leave it alone!"

The ocean carried the thing into shore—closer, closer.

"Yes! Come on!" The boy jumped up and down, waving the thing toward him.

But the water was just teasing. The thing began to float back out.

"No!" The boy stepped into the tide and felt the tug on his toes.

"You'll get dragged in."

"But it's so close." He took a deep breath, then lunged, grabbing a piece of the gray thing in his hand.

"I've got it!" he cried, and turned to escape back up to dry sand.

His foot stepped on a piece of slippery seaweed and slid out from under him. He tried to stay upright, but the water jerked his other leg away. He landed flat on his back in the wet sand.

The low tide crashed over his face.

"Hold on!" he screamed to himself before the ocean filled his mouth.

The water receded, yanking on the boy's wrists and feet. The sand under him slinked away, and he felt himself begin to sink. Fear crawled back into his chest. He was caught. Stuck! He had to get away.

With his fist still clamped around the gray thing, the boy gulped air and closed his eyes. He held his breath as water rushed over him again.

"Trust me. Jump!" The voice floated to the boy, watery and distant. It wasn't the bully or the woman, but someone else—someone angry.

The boy opened his eyes. He wasn't holding the gray thing anymore. His hand was clasped around a metal bar. And instead of sand, he was surrounded by pink rectangular tiles.

"Come on," said the voice. It sounded deep, impatient. "Jump."

A wave beat against him and he gasped, choking in a mouthful of sand. He was back on the beach, stuck in the tide. No more metal bar or pink tiles, just sand and water. And the water tugged at him, the long arms of the monster from the deep pulling the boy into its depths. He couldn't let it take him.

The boy clawed his way out of the tide, dragging the

gray thing behind him. Finally free, he ran back to his favorite spot in the sand. Dry and safe. He lay on his back, his arms and legs sprawled out, soaking in the last rays of the welcoming sun.

He breathed deeply. He had done it. The ocean had tried to take him, tried to suck him down. But he had escaped . . . this time.

He didn't ever want to go near the water again.

He shivered, thinking of its grip on him. And the voice. The angry voice. The pink tiles and the metal bar. Where had they come from? He searched what he could remember, in case it was a memory like the refrigerator, but he couldn't coax more out. Was it something to do with the gray thing?

The boy sat up and pulled the thing onto his lap. "Are you all right?" he asked, straightening the edges, then he frowned. It wasn't an animal at all. He was staring down at a ragged blanket.

"*A blanket!*" The bully laughed. "*You did all that for a blanket?*"

"I like the blanket."

"*You would, baby.*"

The boy ignored the bully's taunt. The blanket didn't give him a clue about the pink tiles, but it still pleased him. "Maybe I have one back home," he said.

"Aww. A little baby with his blanket."

"I'm not a baby. You're just jealous because you can't have it."

"Ha! Yeah, that's what it is."

The boy shook his head and focused on his prize.

The blanket was soggy and frayed but not gray, like he had first thought. It was a very pale blue, like the sky early in the morning before the clouds settled in. The color was masked in places by stains, big purple and brown splotches, like the blanket had been beaten by something much bigger. One corner was torn, another had a great gash, and threads peeled away at the edges. If the boy pulled one, the whole blanket might come apart. He was careful not to pull any.

The cold, wet material was soft between his fingertips, harder in the stained areas. Its smoothness felt familiar; it stirred his heart, but he didn't know why.

All he knew was the blanket comforted him, and for that, he loved it.

FAMILY

THE BLANKET WASN'T BIG, BUT IF THE BOY curled up, it could cover him. It could be his armor, his shield, his protector.

He lifted its middle so the fabric ballooned out below. He smiled. It could be a tent, a giant circus tent for fleas. Or it could be a floppy wizard's cap; he wrapped it around his head with a grin. Or it could be a flag, and he waved it high.

"I claim this beach in the name of King Blanket." He giggled.

Or it could be—

A scuffling noise made the boy jump. Wind riffled the leaves and he dropped the blanket. Was it the beast? The Wolf that maybe lived in the trees? He thought he could smell something awful. Or was it the terrible birds come to attack him again?

He stumbled, tripped, and fell. His heel had caught a rock, partly hidden by sand, and running from it were two crabs, each no longer than his hand. They were so pale in color, they almost blended into the sand. They must've been near the rock, the boy thought, and they must be running from him.

"No, don't go!" He waved at them. "I'm not scary." But the crabs hurried into a hole. They were probably friends. Proper friends, not like the bully and him. Friends who helped each other.

The boy could use a friend.

The scuffling started again, closer this time, and the boy froze. The noise was coming from the rock. The scuffling turned into scraping, and next to the rock, grains of sand flipped into the air, making a tiny, dusty fountain. The boy shuffled backward and stared.

"It won't be good, whatever it is."

"How do you know?" He clenched his fist in case the bully was right.

"Just do. It'll be scary, or terrible—or scary and terrible. You don't want to see it."

The boy's insides twisted. But whatever was making the noise, it had to be small. And he could run from something small.

Down on his knees, he peered around the rock. On the other side, almost out of view, was another crab. It was smaller than the others, barely as long as the boy's finger.

He knelt closer and watched. The fountain sprayed higher as the crab's legs clawed the sand. It was trying to do its sideways dance, but it wasn't going anywhere. One of its legs must have caught under the rock, and now the crab was trapped.

"Told you it'd be terrible."

"It's not terrible," the boy said. "It's cute." He stared at the crab. "Hi." The crab's pincers snapped at the air.

"Watch out! Those things will hurt. Take your finger right off."

"They will?"

"What do you think?"

The boy wasn't sure, but just in case, he stayed back.

This crab was so small, and the words etched in his bones came back to him. *The smaller something is, the more it needs protection.*

"What do you need protection from?" the boy asked the crab. "Not me. I won't hurt you. In fact, I can help you. . . . Maybe."

The boy eyed the raised pincers and itched to run away, but the crab needed his help. He couldn't leave it here alone—like him.

"Once upon a time," the boy whispered, "there was a boy who couldn't be hurt by a crab bite."

He stretched out his hand but quickly pulled back when the crab's pincers came close.

He bit his bottom lip. Now *he* needed help. He turned back to his place on the beach and saw the blanket, lounging on the sand. He smiled thinly, ran to it, then tied two of the corners around his neck and let the fabric flow behind him. It could be a cape.

"The brave knight had hands like steel. . . ." The boy strode to the other side of the rock, away from the crab and its pincers. "And he saved all the crabs in the land from the evil rock monster."

Carefully, the boy wrapped his arms around the rock. He remembered the pain he had felt when he'd pressed down after he first woke up. Would this make it worse? He had to try. Holding his breath, the boy heaved upward. His arm burned, but he kept the rock high until the crab scuttled a few steps away. Then the boy dropped the rock back onto the sand and rubbed the soreness in his arm.

The crab turned to the boy and raised both its pincers, but they didn't snap.

"You're free," the boy said.

The tiny crab didn't move, but the two bigger crabs crept out of their hole. Hurrying to the smaller one with their pincers held high, they corralled the tiny crab across the sand back toward their hole.

Like protectors.

Like parents.

The boy straightened. *Parents.* The crabs were a family.

"We love you." It was the woman's voice again, twirling through the air.

"We miss you, kiddo." And another voice! Deeper. A man. They lit a spark of memory—and the throbbing in his head once more.

"Mom," he whispered, wishing he could concentrate on the voices without the pain. "Dad."

Yes, he had parents! The realization coursed through him as he pushed the pain out of his head. These were their voices. But how could he hear them if they weren't here? Or were they?

"Mom?" he shouted. "Dad?"

But there was nothing. No one. They'd been pulled out of some memory, he guessed. He wished they'd been a solid memory like the refrigerator.

The boy closed his eyes and could feel their love. The way his mother squeezed his hand in hers. The way his father patted his head. He couldn't see them, not clearly. But he could see parts. His mother's dark eyes, and her mouth pulled into a grin so wide, it showed the one crooked tooth that stuck out from the others. His father was more vague. The boy couldn't see his hair or his eyes, just his lips that smiled when he said, "kiddo."

The boy's eyes snapped open.

Was kiddo his name? It felt more familiar than Dude Duds, but . . . The boy shook his head. It wasn't right. Not completely.

Where were his parents now? At their home waiting for him? Out somewhere looking for him?

He closed his eyes and tried to picture them again. Were they tall? Short? Was their hair curly like his? He wished he knew. He wished he could see them, just once. No, if he was going to be honest, he wished he could see them all the time—be with them, touch them, forevermore.

But once would be better than nothing.

"Soon," the boy whispered. They would find him and protect him, just like he had protected the crab.

The boy stood and the parent crabs darted into their hole. But the kid stayed out and stared at its rescuer.

"It's all right," the boy said. "I won't hurt you. You could be my friend. If you want."

"Friends with a crab?"

"He's nicer than you."

The crab peered at the boy . . . then skittered into its home.

The boy was alone again. The cheer he'd felt from saving the crab and remembering his parents drained into the deep sand below his feet.

Even the sun was leaving him. It was kissing the sea good-bye, and the sky had blushed red. The Green Wall was already turning black, just the lit-up eyes blinking in the darkness, but they weren't friends.

The boy had been on the beach for a whole day, and no one had come for him and he had nowhere to go. All he had were wisps of memories, but they weren't a home. He wished he had a hole like the crab family. But he was alone, at night, when any monster could get him.

As the waves snuck up higher, his stomach twisted. He clutched the blanket around him, hoping the waves wouldn't find him in the dark. Hoping his one comfort could protect him.

"You think that's going to save you, some flimsy bit of fabric?"

The boy sighed; he was probably wrong to hope. But the blanket was all he had. It had to help him. He needed it to.

"It's not a blanket; it's a cave," the boy said, pulling the blanket tighter around him. "A pirate cave hidden so well that no thieves can find the treasure."

"*You keep telling yourself that*," the bully said, laughing.

And the boy did. He whispered it deep into the night, as the stars twinkled overhead and the moon watched over him until he finally slept.

A nudge can help shake out memories.
But with fear gripping tightly,
the boy would need direction to move forward.
Something warm.
Something inviting.
Something big.
Perhaps a little comfort would hasten the end.
I watched. I waited.

LIGHT

IN HIS DREAM, THE BOY WAS SUSPENDED, floating in a sky of black. But there were no stars. No moon. Just the darkness, which pulled at him from every direction. Thick blackness that oozed over the boy.

Around him.

Beneath him.

Down his throat.

He woke and coughed, a mouthful of goop gushing onto his chest. *Ewww!* He tried to open his eyes, but they were covered by the grainy sludge too. Swiping at the goopy sand on his face, he cracked his eyes open.

Darkness hung around him. It was still night. But something was different. Something wasn't right. The boy's beating heart told him so.

Cold grasped at his feet. Bony wet fingers creeping up the sand under a giant cloak.

The sea had risen. The monster was trying to take him. To smother him!

"Get back!" he shouted to the sea. To himself. "Get back!"

Wind picked up as he scrambled to his feet, globs of wet sand plopping off him. Something heavy slid off his legs and he caught it quickly. The blanket. He held it close. It had hidden him from the monsters on the land, but nothing could hide from the monster in the sea.

His pulse quickened and the air trembled as the boy scooted to drier sand, back, back until the high tide couldn't reach him. Then he crouched small and pulled the blanket on top of him again.

"Once upon a time, there was a boy who was out of reach," he whispered, glaring at the ocean.

After a few breaths, the water calmed, a soft black comforter, quilted with small, delicate curves. Swaying gently like it hadn't tried to grab him—but the boy knew better.

If his knight had come, he'd have protected the boy, so small against the giant sea. But the boy was still alone.

"Are you there?" he whispered. Even hearing the bully in his head would be better than being alone in the dark.

But it didn't answer.

A line of shimmering white lay over the water, pointing to where the moon hung low in the sky, big and round, but not quite full, like a cake covered in white frosting with one side sliced off. And above, the stars winked at him. He gave them a small smile. Perhaps they were protecting him. Perhaps they had sent away the wind and put the slimy old monster back to sleep in the sea.

Could they bring back the sun?

The boy sighed, wishing he were still asleep. But when he closed his eyes, the blackness of his dream rushed back to him. Staying awake was better.

He listened for danger, but all he heard was the *shush-shush* of the tide grasping for higher land, then receding. He tucked his chin against his chest and pulled his knees in tighter. If he was small, maybe nothing would see him, nothing would harm him. It was dark, after all.

Until the light appeared.

It came from his left. At first he thought it was a reflection from the moon—

But it was too bright. It couldn't be the sunrise, either. The sun lit up the whole sky, but this was a single ray, like a beam from an enormous flashlight.

It shone from the northeast. Yes, the boy knew that! The sun went from the east to the west, so this light was from the northeast.

For a few seconds, the light shone on the beach, the trees, and the boy. He squinted against the brightness, which carved a path through the dark. Then it was gone.

Everything went black and gray again, with only the moonlight illuminating the shoreline and trees the boy was cradled between.

He sat up and searched for the light. Where had it gone? Would it come back?

Please come back, he thought.

"Did you see?" he whispered, but the bully didn't reply.

The boy waited—still small, still invisible. His breath skipped across his lips. He closed his eyes and crossed all his fingers. Please. Please. PLEASE!

And it came again.

When the boy saw the ray, he forgot all about the dark, the monsters, the invading sea. He jumped up and grinned.

It was a broad swath of light—yellowish white, like it was old and warm. The light swung to the north and lifted the boy's heart as it went.

Then it was gone. He was alone once more.

"Where are you? Where did you come from?" he called to the empty sky.

But there was no response. He waited, waited, but this time the light did not return.

He dropped back onto the ground, pulling his head into his shoulders. Silence and darkness swallowed him.

JOURNEY

THE SUN'S WARMTH KISSED THE BOY GOOD
morning. He stretched his arms and legs, then yelped as
his toe collided with a tree.

"Horrible tree." He stood and kicked it with his other
foot.

Then the warning scurried up from the pit of his stomach: Shadows. Noises. Eyes. He was beside the Green
Wall!

Clouds passed over the sun, dropping the beach into
shadow. The boy grabbed the blanket and hurried to the
center of the sand, grateful the intruding water had now
retreated.

The beach looked the same this morning, beautiful
but still dangerous.

But the boy knew *he* was different. He felt buoyant.
His fear still stirred within him, but he had survived the
night. No monsters had eaten him. And today he would
be rescued. He was sure of it.

He had seen that light. He had hope.

He searched for the light again. Above the trees hung a pale blue sky. Wispy clouds drifted silently. Silhouettes of birds waltzed to unsung music. But there was no beam of light.

"That's okay," the boy told himself. He had seen it—twice. And he had woken with an assurance rising from deep in his belly that his parents were searching for him. They must've sent the light. They'd be here soon and he wouldn't have to worry about monsters anymore. He wouldn't even have to worry about finding food, because they'd take him home and give him whatever he wanted.

He knew it. Almost to the bottom of his toes.

One thing bothered him: The light hadn't stopped when it passed over. If it had seen him, wouldn't it have stopped? Wouldn't it have marked the place where his parents could find him?

The bully tapped on his brain. The boy wanted to ignore it. He knew what it was going to say, and he didn't want to hear the words.

But the bully was persistent.

"No one is coming."

"Go away," the boy whispered.

But it didn't go away. *"No one is coming."*

"Go away!" the boy said louder.

But it wouldn't go away. *"No one is coming."*

"GO AWAY!"

An explosion erupted behind him. The boy ducked his head as hundreds of birds filled the sky above. This time he wasn't so afraid; his heart was filled with too much sorrow from being lost and alone. He watched them through squinting eyes. Beating wings. Screeching voices. They didn't grow big. They didn't come close. They didn't even look at him. They just flitted back and forth, chattering noisily.

What's that kid doing here? the boy imagined they were saying. *Why doesn't he go home?*

Tears blurred his sight, but he pushed them away. He sniffed back the thickness building in his nose. He would not cry.

The bully couldn't be right. It just couldn't.

"You know I'm right. No one is coming."

A sob escaped. The boy couldn't stop it. But he squashed the rest of the snivels that were right behind.

It had been a day and a half since he'd been born on the beach. Someone would've come by now if they knew he was here. Surrounded by sand, trees, and water. With no one close enough to hear him scream. He was small. If they knew where he was, they would've protected him. And if they'd seen him with the light, it wouldn't have left.

He rubbed the tears from his face and stomped his foot, sending tiny flecks of sand into the air.

"Fine!" he said. "Fine! Fine! Fine! Fine! FINE!"

He didn't want to say, *You're right*, but he figured the bully already knew he was thinking it.

"Fine, no one is coming."

Saying it aloud, even as a whisper, made it real—not just the words, but the frightful dread that had been bubbling quietly in his gut since he had woken up on this deserted beach. Now, no gulping or holding his breath or pinching his thigh could keep it back. The tidal wave welled up inside him. It crashed in his chest, forcing his body onto the sand. He wrapped his arms around his stomach, hoping for any comfort.

He cried.

When all his tears had left him, the boy lay on his side, staring out at the endless ocean. He felt empty, spent.

He rubbed his lip with the edge of his finger. The bully was right. No one was coming. If his parents knew where he was, they wouldn't have shined a light to find him.

The boy sat up. That's right! The light. *I should go to*

the light, he thought. *That's where I'll find my parents.* His heart skipped. Yes, that was what he had to do.

But the boy lay back down on the sand, listening to the lapping surf and chirping birds, watching the clouds peer at him as they sailed far above, feeling his stomach clench inside him.

He knew he wasn't safe on this beach, but if he left, he could be . . .

     stuck by the rocks . . .

          caught in the trees . . .

               dragged down, down, down by the

                    water . . .

"Coward."

"I don't care what you call me."

"Oh yes, you do. Coward."

The boy sat up again in protest. "I'm being smart. You don't just go out on a quest. You have to plan for it."

"A quest? You're not a knight. You can't even get past those rocks."

A knight. Yes, he needed to be a knight. "If I were a knight, I'd have a suit of armor and I could walk over those rocks with no problem."

"But you're not a knight. You don't even know where you're going."

"I'm going to the light. It's that way." He pointed, in case the bully didn't remember. "I'm going to my parents."

"Ha. For all you know, they've already left."

"They wouldn't leave without me!"

"The light didn't find you last night, did it? They probably gave up."

The boy lay down again. The bully had a point. What if he got to the light and no one was there? There was still a chance that someone could find him here, if he stayed. He *had* survived the night, after all. He might be able to do it again.

"Yeah, see? If you leave, you won't know what's out there. You won't have anywhere to sleep. Nah, you were right the first time; you should *stay here. You're* not *a knight. You can't do it."*

The boy sighed. What was he thinking? Of course he wasn't a knight. He was small and needed protection.

So why did his heart want him to go?

He pulled the blanket around him and lifted the torn corner to rub his lip for comfort, but a strange pattern on the fabric caught the boy's eye: a horizontal line, with three shorter lines extending down. It was too precise to be a stain. And its red color was different from any other area of the blanket. Was it a picture of a table, or a three-legged stool? No, that didn't seem right.

The boy cocked his head, raised the corner up to the sun for a better look. He turned it slowly and gasped. From this side, the picture was clear: *E*. A big red *E* in the corner. And now that he looked closer, there were other red lines too, and swirls. Some were faded. Was it an *H*? Maybe an *N*? What did the marks mean?

Maybe it was a name, the name of whoever owned the blanket. A person on a ship, maybe. Or . . .

His heart danced and he sprang up. "A hotel! The blanket must've come from a hotel. With another beach, filled with umbrellas and loungers and sand castles and people. People!"

That was where his parents were, and even if they had given up, the other people would be able to help him get home.

The beach couldn't be far. The blanket probably followed the coast here, to him.

Hope filled his chest like a balloon. He felt like he could float above the rocks, above the Green Wall of trees.

He wished he could float to the Umbrella Beach.

"No luck for you. You'll have to walk there, with the rocks, the beast, the water, all the scary things coming—"

"All right!"

The boy stared up the coast. The sand glinted in the sun like a yellow brick road, beckoning him on.

The Umbrella Beach—where the light was, where his parents were—was close. So close. He knew it in his heart. And he knew, hoped, his parents wouldn't leave without him. They had told him they loved him. They'd sent the light. And maybe they'd sent the blanket, too. He had to try to get to them.

The boy gazed around to make sure he wasn't leaving anything behind. He patted his pockets. The scrap of fabric was in its usual place. Other than that, he had nothing else to take.

"You won't make it. Everything's scary. You said so yourself."

The boy tightened the knot of the blanket around his neck. It had protected him during the night. And he thought of the crab, his friend, if only for a few seconds. He had helped the crab. He had been a knight then.

"Not everything's scary," the boy said, scrunching up his fear like used paper. "If you're scared, then *you* stay. I'm going to the Umbrella Beach."

He flung the blanket over his shoulders and glanced around for the last time at the sand, water, and trees, this place where he had first woken up—where he had been born. Then, holding his fear deep inside, he strode across the sand. This time no rocks appeared. The path opened up to him like an invitation.

He walked away from all that he knew, onward toward the sun.

MOUNTAIN

IT WASN'T LONG BEFORE THE BOY COULDN'T see the beach where he had been born at all. Just a stream of yellow sand running along the coast behind him. Waves crashed on one side and the impenetrable Green Wall chased him on the other.

Drops of water leaped up to pull him to the ocean, but he dodged out of their reach. As the path curved around the coast, he kept to the middle, as far away from both his fears as possible.

He couldn't let anything stop him. He had to get to the Umbrella Beach. He had to get to his parents. He had to get home fast, before one of the scary things here ate him.

The sun hurried the boy along too, rising to its highest point quickly then beginning to descend. The boy tried to slow it, telling the sun stories of knights who slayed dragons, battled legions, and rode across deserts to get home to their family. He pretended he was the knight, slashing across the land, but he knew the hero knights had something he didn't, and he was reminded every time his stomach grumbled.

Chirp!

He halted.

Ahead a small bird perched on a root sticking up at the edge of the Green Wall. Something pink oozed out of its beak, and the boy winced. It must've been eating a worm, he thought. *Yuck!*

"*Better turn back,*" the bully said. "*Don't want that bird to turn terrible.*"

"You think it will?"

"*Maybe it'll eat you like it's eating that worm.*"

The bird's claw picked up whatever it was eating from the ground, and the boy could see that it wasn't a worm. It looked like some kind of seed.

"What is that?" the boy said, clutching the corner of the blanket. He stepped closer and—

"*Don't get too close.*"

Too late. The bird twitched its head, then unfolded its wings and flew. The boy jumped back, but the bird glided into the sky and behind the Green Wall. The boy took a breath, then stalked over to the root and peered at the bird's meal. It was a small purple ball, about the size of a puffed-up grape, covered in a leathery skin, except for where the bird had bitten into it. Inside was a brown pit, surrounded by a layer of pink jelly.

"If this is okay for the birds, it must be okay for me," he said, picking up the ball for a closer inspection.

"Who says?"

"Isn't it?"

"I don't know. If you're such a genius, eat it. If it's poisonous, you'll figure it out soon enough."

"Poisonous!"

The boy clapped his hand over his mouth. He had said the word too loudly. He hoped the horrible beast in the Green Wall hadn't followed him. But the trees stayed silent. Nothing moved. He turned back to examine the grape thing and whispered, "You think so?"

"I've been here as long as you have," the bully said. *"How should I know?"*

The boy's stomach grumbled again. Maybe it knew something his head didn't, that these grape things—sea grapes, maybe, as they were by the sea—were fine for people. They looked all right. In fact, they looked like they might taste good.

"I think they're perfect," the boy said, shooing his doubt away.

"Suit yourself."

The boy found more grapes, ones that had not yet been bitten. He picked up a large one that looked juicy and carefully wiped the sand off its hard, rough skin. He brought it to his lips, but a thought stopped him: *Maybe bugs crawled on it.* He rubbed the grape hard on his T-shirt to clean off any invisible bug prints.

He lifted it to his lips again, then gathered his courage and took in a long, deep breath—in case it would be his last.

When his teeth finally sank through the flesh, the sweet jelly swam over his tongue.

"Taste good?"

"Mm-hmm."

"Not poisonous then?" The bully sounded unconvinced.

The boy shook his head. "Uh-uh."

He spun the hard pit around in his mouth so his teeth could scrape off every last morsel. When the pit was clean, he spat it on the sand, tossed the skin away and tried another grape. It tasted even better.

The sea grapes had come from the tree next to him. Branches hung over the sand, dangling large circular leaves, and—high above his head—they cradled thick bunches of sea grapes. They were too high for the boy to reach, but he found plenty more on the ground. Ignoring the pain that kept twitching in his arm, the boy stuffed handfuls of the sea grapes into his pockets, then pulled out the bottom of his T-shirt to capture even more.

Some of the wide leaves closer to him were upturned like expectant palms, and they were filled with water, probably from a rain not long ago. The boy tilted one to his mouth and laughed as the liquid ran down his throat. He drank from another and another, until no part of him felt thirsty anymore.

Biting into sea grapes, he continued his journey, a smile drifting onto his face. He'd found water and food.

By the time the sun was halfway down the sky, his belly was satisfied, but his fear was not. His yellow path was so narrow that the Green Wall almost trampled the coast. The boy was trapped on a thin line of sand between the dense trees and the wide ocean. Panic squeezed his heart, but he tried to ignore it. He had to keep going.

"Feet straight ahead," he told himself. "Focus on the Umbrella Beach."

But the coast turned sharply, and the boy stopped dead. Ahead, a boulder rose up like a giant fist, blocking his path. The darkness of the Green Wall hugged one side of the boulder, and angry waves punched the other. The only way for the boy to continue was to go over, but

the boulder was at least three times bigger than him—
and grew taller the longer he stared.

"You're in trouble now." The bully's words were lined
with a sneer.

The boy gulped. "No trouble," he said, hiding his shaking hand in his pocket. "I just have to climb it."

He tried to grasp the rock with his fingers. But the surface was too smooth and slippery; it had no crevices or
cracks where he could place his toes to hoist himself up.
The boy jumped but just slid back down again.

The boulder might as well be a mountain.

"You can just go over it, huh?"

"Shut up."

He crumpled onto the ground and leaned his back
against the cold, hard barrier.

*"Well, that's that. Told you we shouldn't have left the
beach."*

He crossed his arms. "I'm not giving up. I have to get
to my parents."

*"You might as well give up. You're not getting past this
thing. And let's face it, there's no way you're brave enough to
go into those trees. And the ocean? You'll never survive."*

The boy shrank into himself, arms pulling his knees
tight into his chest. He stared out at the water, at the

waves that plowed toward him from the horizon, building and building, reaching and reaching, until they launched against the side of the boulder and broke into a million drops. He knew they were searching for him. If he tried to go around the boulder by the sea, the waves would capture him, drag him,

down . . .

down . . .

down to the monster below.

He couldn't let them get him. He had to stay away from the water.

But he couldn't go through the Green Wall, either. He hadn't seen any more of the terrible birds, only normal small birds, but that didn't mean they couldn't change at any minute. And what about the hissing, the wolf beast? He had seen the twinkling eyes, heard the cracking twigs, smelled the stench of . . . something.

He knew that he couldn't stay on the thin strip of sand and rock, either. The tide had already risen, just since he'd stopped here. Soon the waves would break over the rocky coast and devour what was left of the sandy pathway— devour him. There was nothing the boy could do to stop it. There was nowhere to hide. Even the blanket wouldn't be able to help him now.

"Yep. Thought so. You should just go back. Or give up. You know you're going to. Might as well get it over with."

The boy set his jaw, shooed away the bully's words. He stared at the line of trees, so dark and deep. A hoot, a squeak, a creak crept out. He scooted farther away, but he was inches from the hungry sea.

Going through that line of trees—and facing whatever they were hiding—was the only way to get to his parents. It was his only hope.

He had been brave before. He'd helped the crab, and followed the light. He had a cape just like the knight from the fridge door, but maybe it would help if he had a sword. Yes, with a sword, the boy could beat back any beasts— even a bear with a wolf's head.

The sand under the boy's feet was covered in thick roots that crawled out from under the Green Wall and twigs that had dropped from the tops of the trees. Near the base of the boulder, he found a stick about the length of his arm. It was thin and blunt—not much of a sword—but it was something.

He adjusted the knot of the blanket around his neck, arranged the fabric on his shoulders. With the sword leaning on the boulder next to him, the boy crossed his arms and puffed out his chest. "I am a knight. A pirate knight," he told the ocean, the Green Wall, the world. "I will fight anything."

Nothing questioned his toughness. Not even the bully.

Still, the boy dropped his arms and sighed. He wasn't sure he even believed himself. But he had to try.

With his hands shaking, he turned to the trees and raised his stick. He stepped through the Green Wall.

Courage showed promise.
His love drove him.
But fear doesn't give up.
It feeds when people try to be brave.
It grows when people doubt.
And when what they love most
is what makes them most afraid,
the outcome is almost certain.
I had hope, but it was a treasure I was sure would be stolen.
I watched. And I waited.

GREEN WALL

THE OTHER SIDE OF THE GREEN WALL WAS different from what the boy had expected. It was darker than the beach, but not as black as it looked from outside. Sharp rays of light bore down between the trees, illuminating a parade of colors. Leaves gleamed every shade of green, brown, and gray. Blurs of red and blue twittered in the treetops.

Even the air was different. It was cooler and smelled cleaner than the salty air on the beach. *Because of the trees,* the boy thought, a fragment of a memory coming to him, then flitting away again.

There were a lot of trees. Trunk after trunk after trunk, rising out of the ground and into the sky. Every one had branches that crisscrossed over one another, fighting for their own space and piece of sun. The growth was so thick that after only a short distance, the boy couldn't see the rocks or the ocean anymore. With every step he took, the forest opened in front of him and silently closed behind.

What he liked most was that he was walking away from the hungry, angry sea. Before long, the boy couldn't even hear the waves breaking on the shore. He was safe from the long fingers of the tide.

But he knew that didn't mean he was safe from everything. It was quieter here. And that made every sudden noise more scary. Twigs snapped. Leaves rustled. Wind whispered. The forest seemed to breathe.

"Don't be afraid," the boy murmured to the blanket, and wiped his sweaty palms on his shorts.

He tried to keep his mind off all the things that scared him. He thought about Umbrella Beach and seeing his parents for the first time. They'd raise their arms, smile, and shout . . . What would they shout? What would they call him? Why did he know frogs were making that croaking noise and about hotels and umbrellas and loungers, but he couldn't picture his parents and he didn't even know the most important thing about himself—his name?

That question kept itching to be asked. But he didn't want to admit that he still couldn't remember his own name. It haunted the boy, toyed with him. A whisper on the edge of his hearing. So close, but just out of reach. And yet, it was something he should know.

Laughter broke out. *"It's amazing you even know how to walk."*

"Leave me alone," the boy said. He walked faster, then realized he couldn't get away from this bully.

"How about I help you remember? Your name is . . . Drake the snake."

"No, it's not."

"Shane the stain?"

"Stop it!"

"Stu the poo?"

The boy gritted his teeth and banged his hand on his temple.

"Remember!" he demanded.

His brain didn't respond, so the boy banged harder.

"Remember! Remember! REMEMBER!"

His brain still returned nothing—except a small pain in his temple.

"Unnhh."

"Forget it," the bully said. *"Oh yeah. You already have."*

The boy put his hands over his ears. But it didn't keep the bully out.

"Good thing your head's screwed on tight or you might forget—"

"SHUT UP!" The boy halted. Angry breaths charged

out of his mouth, and his hands clenched into fists at his side. He waited, breathing and listening, expecting the bully to taunt him again, but it was quiet.

"Good," the boy said. "Stay away."

He strode on, trying to focus on the crackle of dry leaves under his feet, waving away the tiny flies that buzzed around his face, pretending not to see the spiders that peered at him from sticky webs. The more he walked, the more the shadows played with him, hiding behind tree trunks, running in front, then stretching out along the pathway ahead.

But the boy barely noticed. He couldn't ignore the anger that had built up inside him. It wasn't his fault he couldn't remember his name; at least, he didn't think it was. It wasn't as though he didn't want to know his name. To hear his parents say it. To be with them and not alone in this place with the scary water and trees and monsters. It wasn't as though he wasn't trying.

The question was: Would trying be enough?

He remembered the way his father's voice had called him kiddo. The boy knew that wasn't his real name, could feel it down to his toes, but perhaps it was a special name his father called him. A name his dad used when the boy had done something good or made him proud.

He wondered if his father would be proud of him now.

The boy hoped he would. He wished he could see his father, even in a memory, know what they did together. He felt that he wanted to show his father . . . he wasn't sure what, but he suddenly longed to show his father something—

A rustle. A branch snapped. Leaves crunched.

The boy froze.

Fear erupted in his stomach. His breath caught in his throat. He had been reckless, moving too noisily and shouting at the bully when he should've kept quiet.

Before he even turned, the boy knew what was behind him.

He wished he didn't.

BEAST

A TERRIBLE ROAR SHOOK THE WHOLE FOREST. The boy dropped onto his knees and slammed his hands over his ears. But it was too late. The sound had crawled inside his brain, echoing on and on and on.

Gusts blew up around him, tossing and tumbling the Green Wall. On top of the roar, squeals and squawks raced into his ears, and creaks and cracks darted straight to his heart. The boy curled up tight, held out his stick, and opened one eye.

It stood tall between the trees.

Hunched on its two back legs.

Shrouding the boy in its shadow.

It was like the boy had imagined—the body of a huge bear with the head of a terrifying wolf—but it was worse. It towered over him, black hair tinged with gray ruffled in the wind. Muscles rippled under its skin. Ears twitched at every noise. And a scar weaved across its face.

The beast had fought before.

And it had won.

Long, shining claws, ragged from destroying prey. Yellow teeth, sharp, dripped with drool. Bright green eyes glowed and stared through the boy.

"No," the boy whimpered. "Please, no."

The beast stretched out its paws, its knuckles cracking.

"Once upon a time," the boy whispered, "there was a boy who saw the biggest beast in all the land, and the boy . . ." The beast snorted, his teeth bared.

"RAN!"

The boy scrambled up and fled as fast as he could, shoving branches away from his face. He didn't follow a path but ran wherever the trees where thickest, so the beast couldn't see him. Wind shrieked around him, and he pushed against it to keep moving forward, to escape.

He ran and ran and ran. Until his breath was heavy and his feet were sore. He ran until he couldn't hear anything except his own heartbeat pounding in his ears.

He slid behind a thick trunk and peered all around.

The beast was nowhere to be seen. Not a hair. Not a footstep. Not a drop of drool. It hadn't come after the boy, or he had outrun it. Either way, it wouldn't kill him now. He was safe.

But for how long?

"You're never going to be safe. You'll always be afraid." The

boy had known the bully wouldn't stay silent for long.

"I . . . just . . . saved . . . you . . . from . . . the . . . beast, didn't I?" the boy said, each word coming out between ragged breaths. He bent over, holding his shaking hands against his belly.

"It'll find you. A beast like that will be able to smell you and hunt you down."

Gulping more air, the boy straightened and tried to build up his courage. "I'll run to the Umbrella Beach. It won't catch me."

"You see any sign of a beach around here?"

His shoulders slumped. He didn't want the bully to be right, but all he could see were trees. He couldn't even hear the crash of waves on the shore. He couldn't be near Umbrella Beach yet.

And worst, the sky was starting to darken.

Had all this been a mistake? Would the beast have come after him if he'd stayed on the beach? Was he right to follow the light?

Uncertainty pressed against his gut; he wished there was some way he could know for sure.

Then a twinkle flickered at the corner of his eye and his heart flew. Perhaps the light had come to find him again.

But it wasn't the giant beam he had seen the night

before; it was a tiny spark of light flittering between the branches of the trees. The boy watched it, trailing its path as it danced around the trunks and across the ground.

Another spark blossomed beside him, then spun off to play in the leaves. Then another, and another, until there were thousands of tiny sparks of light glimmering around the path before him.

The boy smiled. "Fireflies," he whispered, and as if recognizing their own name, the glowing bugs jumped. He laughed and lifted his arms so the fireflies could waltz around them. Then the sparks all rose high in the sky and dove back down in a glittering cloud.

"'She perfumed my planet and lit up my life.'" The words drifted out from behind the fireflies, sweet and kind. "'I should never have run away.'"

It was his mother's voice! The boy's smile bloomed.

"Mom, I'm here. Where are you?" he called, and the fireflies pirouetted outward. Behind them, the boy saw a large hump of pale blue that glowed from inside.

"Mom?" He hesitated, but the hump fluttered, lifting the front. It was a makeshift tent, and under it sat a woman—his mother! He had finally found her. A child sat next to her, and they both stared at a book on her lap, the pages illuminated by her flashlight.

"Mom!" the boy called, but she didn't look up.

She stroked the hair of the child next to her and read, "'In order to make his escape I believe he took advantage of a migration of wild birds.'"

The boy's heart leaped. *The Little Prince*! He remembered that book, and the part where the Little Prince was carried away from his planet with strings attached to birds.

"Mom! It's me. I found you."

He ran to his mother, but the fireflies descended once more, so many of them that he couldn't see. He raised his arms in front of his face as he plowed through the fireflies, but when he got to the spot where she'd been, it was empty. His mother was gone.

"NO! Come back!"

He collapsed on his knees, scrabbling in the dead leaves for some sign of her, but there was none.

"Please. Mom."

Only the fireflies answered him, flittering away until he was alone again in the dying day.

The boy sat on his heels, his blanket over his back and his stick at his side. He fought back tears as he touched the place where his mother had been. No, not his mother, just a memory of her. And the boy was him! His younger self. He could see it clearly in his mind now; they'd been camping in their backyard, a sheet for a tent, and she'd read almost every book he owned with a flashlight to see the words.

A light like the one she sent to find him and bring him to Umbrella Beach.

His heart ached to have her back, but he did find comfort. His memory was a sign that he was going the right way. When he reached Umbrella Beach, he'd thank her for the stories, for the sign, for the light.

But when would that be?

The boy stood up, brushing dead leaves off his shins. He arranged the blanket around his shoulders, ready to get back to his journey. To get to Umbrella Beach.

But the playful shadows had grown black and thick. The trees were silhouettes now, and the sky was on fire.

"*Your friend Darkness is coming,*" the bully said.

"So?" the boy replied, trying to control the uncertain waver in his voice.

"*Better do something quick. Night won't wait.*"

It didn't seem right that the sun was already saying good night. Had it really been a whole day since the boy had left his beach? He didn't feel tired—yet, as he thought of it, tiredness crashed on top of him, weighted him down.

He couldn't go on. He didn't want to be without his

parents for one more night, but the Umbrella Beach wasn't close and he couldn't chance the wolf-beast finding him in the dark, when he wouldn't be able to see.

He pushed away his disappointment, gulped down his fear, and looked around for a place where he could stay safe for the night. A place where the beast couldn't find him.

But there was nowhere to hide. Even if he snuggled up to a trunk, the beast could easily get him.

He wished he had his mother's tent, tied up between two trees. But maybe . . . A star winked at him through the leaves overhead. *Yes,* it seemed to say. *You know what to do.*

The boy nodded. He *did* know what to do.

Leaving his stick at the base of the tree, he grabbed the nearest branch and hoisted himself up. The injury inside his arm protested, but he ignored it. He pulled up. Then again. And again. He had climbed trees before; the movements felt familiar. His hands found the strongest branches, and his toes curled around the deep grooves in the bark. Before long, he was high up in the tree, cradled in the V between the trunk and a thick branch. Far above anything that could harm him. Far above the wolf.

He didn't look down—his gut told him he shouldn't. But he did look out.

Up here, the leaves were thinner. The sky was blushing and the sun sat on its last perch above the horizon.

The boy was once again spending a night alone, and his insides felt hollow. He thought about the memory he'd seen with his mother reading to him and wondered if she'd ever read to him again.

"*Hmm hmmmm hmm hmmm, hmmmm hmmmmm. Hmm hmmmm hmm hmmm.*"

A song danced with the wind through the treetops, and the boy tilted his head so he could hear it better. The tune reminded him of something. He wasn't sure what, but he didn't care. It warmed his heart.

"*Hmm hmmmm hmm hmmm, hmmmm hmmmmm. Hmm hmmmm hmm hmmm.*"

He hummed along too. "*Hmm hmmmm hmm hmmm.*" Then said, "'Here Comes the Sun'! I know this song. My mom likes it. . . . Mom?"

His heart soared, but the throb in his head returned. He narrowed his eyes against the pain.

The voice hummed again, lower this time, like it was laced with something else . . . sadness, the boy thought.

"Mom!" he called louder, driving the pain away so he could hear better.

But the song was gone.

It had sounded so real, so close, but it must've been just a wisp of memory that had bubbled up from a corner of his mind, and the pain had kept it at bay. He wished it would come back, but he continued the song.

As he untied the blanket from around his neck and carefully spread it over himself, he sang the words over and over, and they lifted him.

Leaning back, he stuffed his hand into his pocket and pulled out three sea grapes. The sun would come back soon, and tomorrow he'd find the Umbrella Beach and his parents. He had to.

As he swallowed the sweet jelly, he watched the sun drown.

NIGHT

SLEEP CAME EASILY FOR THE BOY THIS TIME. He was so tired, his eyes closed as soon as the sun said good-bye. He snuggled into sleep's welcoming arms and was hugged close, until his fears took hold.

Water haunted his dreams again. Thick, oppressive water that slipped around him and held him prisoner. It pulled at his ankles, his knees, his chest. He tried to breathe, to call for help. But he was sucked—

down,

down,

down.

The water swallowed his scream.

The boy's eyes jerked open as he sat up, hitting his head on a branch.

"A dream," he whispered. "Just a dream."

His hand shook against his thigh, and he held it still.

The boy was still sitting in the tree, but now he was surrounded by a black ink sky, with not even the moon or stars visible. Thick, dark clouds crowded overhead, blocking out anything friendly.

The night brought new sounds: buzzing, chirping, croaking. "Just insects and frogs," the boy told the blanket. But he couldn't ignore the snapping of twigs below. Something was moving down there, and he hoped he was wrong about what it was.

He wanted to go back to sleep, to escape the scary darkness. But sleep wouldn't come now. Every time he closed his eyes, his ears picked up some far-off noise. Monsters searching for him, he was sure. The giant Wolf with its scar and sharp teeth, or maybe the creeping ocean, just like in his dreams.

Even up here, high in the tree, he didn't feel safe. Not really. He had his blanket, but if they looked up, any monsters could see him sitting on this branch. He hoped they couldn't get this high.

The clouds snuck in lower, and the wind started to whistle in the trees.

The boy crept farther under his blanket. Were those scratches he could hear below? Sloshing waves? He tried to look, but when he bent over, the height made his stomach turn.

"*Don't do that. Are you dense or something? Forget it; I already know.*"

The boy breathed deeply, trying to steady his shaking hand.

"I shouldn't be here," he said.

"*You were the one who thought it was a good idea to leave the beach.*"

"I mean I shouldn't be *here*," the boy said, "in this place, wherever it is. I should be at the Umbrella Beach, with my parents and . . . whoever else is looking for me. I should be drinking soda and eating cake and pizza, and having fun. Not here, in this tree, with you."

He kicked the trunk so hard, it rocked the branch he was sitting on. His heart leaped as he held on tight, trying not to topple down to the ground. The wind picked up and the clouds closed in tighter.

"*How do you know your parents are even there?*"

"What do you mean?"

"*Do you have any proof?*"

"I saw the light, dummy. I found this blanket."

"*I mean real proof.*"

The boy didn't respond. The blanket and the light were good enough for him.

Except that he hadn't seen the light for a while. Not since last night, when he was still on the beach. Maybe . . .

"*They're not looking for you.*"

No.

But maybe . . .

"*You're even more lost now.*"

No!

But maybe . . .

"*They've gone home.*"

"NOOOOOOO!"

CLAP!

Thunder cracked over the boy's head. Lightning streaked out of the clouds above.

The branches shook. The boy's eyes shot open as he grabbed the tree's trunk.

"What was that?"

The wind answered, battering the leaves and howling through the forest.

The boy trembled. He did what his stomach told him not to—he looked down. And immediately wished he hadn't. He was so high up, and the ground was so far away. He was in the middle of the sky.

He hoped the sky wasn't falling.

"Mom," he whispered, but she didn't reply. He wished her words would come back, the ones in the air. So he wasn't . . .

"Alone.

"With me.

"And all the monsters."

The boy cowered.

Water splattered his cheek. Squeezing the trunk with one arm, he wiped his face. Was it the ocean? Could it reach him up here?

Water splashed on the blanket. His arms. His legs.

He turned his eyes up. Each raindrop looked like a tiny bullet coming straight for him.

"Better run."

It was still dark, and the boy could barely see. He couldn't climb back down to the ground. The Wolf might be there, waiting for him. No, he'd be safe in the tree. He hoped he'd be safe in the tree.

"I'm staying here." The boy curled up tight against the trunk, burying his head beneath the blanket. But it couldn't keep out the rain or the noise of the storm.

CRACK!

A flash of light pierced the dark. But it wasn't his parents' light. Their light was warm and welcoming. This light was cold. Very cold.

BOOM!

Thunder rocked the tree.

"You wanna run now, don't you?"

The boy dug his chin deeper into his chest. His branch was sturdy, but not so thick that he couldn't be thrown off. And what if that lightning got closer? What if it scorched the tree—and everything on it? His heart quaked with terrible possibilities. He shouldn't stay, but he was frozen.

Wind whipped past his face, slapping his head against the trunk. He held on tighter.

CRACK! BOOM!

Each burst of lightning lit up the branches around him. Like fingers pointing, eyes staring, teeth glinting— ready to dig into the boy. They disappeared into the black night. Reappeared with every crack.

The boy held his breath, letting it out in each brief reprieve. When the thunder was gone, he could hear only the rain. The birds and insects and frogs in the forest were all silent now, hiding safely in nooks and crannies.

"Hooo."

Except one.

The boy peered around the edge of the blanket. At the end of his branch sat a small owl, a baby. Its eyes were wide open, its ears pricked up. Its whole body trembled.

The boy stared at it.

"What are you doing? Fly away. Hide."

The owl stared back. Rain pelted its feathers. Wind shoved it along the branch.

"Get somewhere safe," the boy shouted. But the owl didn't move.

The boy buried his head again, water streaming down his face. He closed his eyes, wishing for his mother. She'd know what to do; she'd know how to help the owl. She'd help them both. He pictured his mother the way he had just seen her, surrounded by fireflies and reading *The Little Prince*. He wished he were the Little Prince; the prince had protected the rose, put a glass cover over her to keep her safe from the wind. But the boy . . .

He peered out of the blanket again.

"Hooo."

The wind was so strong, the owl was barely holding on to the branch. It shivered against the gale rushing past. The boy shivered too. Fear grew in the owl's big round eyes. A mirror of his own.

They needed protection, a roof, four walls. Shelter.

CRACK! BOOM!

Lightning flashed, and something caught the boy's eye a few trees away. Wood, but not round branches. Wooden planks laid out like a floor, covered by a thick layer of leaves for a roof and sides.

A tree house.

STORM

A TREE HOUSE? IN THIS FOREST?

The boy shook his head, blinked hard, and pinched his thigh.

The tree house was still there!

If he could get the owl behind those walls, they'd have shelter. They'd be safe.

The boy had helped the crab. Could he help the owl, too?

"Do you seriously think you can save that? You can't even save yourself."

"It needs my help."

"Just because it needs you doesn't mean you can help."

The tree house was not in the boy's tree. To get to it, he'd have to climb down his tree. In the rain. With the thunder. And who knew if the beast was waiting at the bottom.

"It's a long way down."

"I don't need you to tell me that."

Wind whistled by his ears. Raindrops pricked his skin.

"You might fall."

"I know."

CRACK! BOOM!

The boy stiffened.

"That's right. Stay here. It's the easiest thing to do. And you know you want to do the easiest thing. After all, it's only a thunderstorm . . . with lightning . . . that could strike you."

"Shut up."

The boy searched for a trail he could follow to the tree house. The branch he was balancing on led to another one, a thicker one. He could climb to there, then shimmy to the next. That branch intersected with a thinner one. Could he balance on it? It would only be for one step. Just so he could reach that limb on the next tree over. Then he'd be below the tree house and could climb into it, into safety.

"Once upon a time, there was a boy who climbed like a monkey."

He turned to the owl. It was still staring, still trembling.

"It's going to be okay." The boy tried to keep his voice calm. "I'm coming to get you."

He brushed the water from his face, then pulled the blanket off himself. He hated that it was getting wet, but he needed it. He tied two corners under his chin, pulled the knot behind his neck, then tucked the bottom of the blanket into the waistband of his shorts so it formed a pocket by his belly.

CRACK! BOOM!

The boy froze, hesitated. The owl blinked.

"Hooo."

"Once upon a time," the boy said, "there was a boy who saved all the creatures in the land." He crawled along the branch, his arm outstretched until his hand curled around the baby owl. Its feathers were soft and delicate.

"You'll be fine," the boy said, hoping he believed it. "We're going over there."

He pointed at the tree house—so close, but also so far away—then he placed the owl under the blanket.

"Hold on, okay?"

"You think it's going to be safe in there?"

"It better be."

The boy took a deep breath and stepped out of his cradle. Rain pummeled his skin as his fingers grasped for the next branch. His toes gripped the damp wood. He closed his eyes, pictured himself and the owl inside, sheltered by those leaves, safe.

He shifted his weight. He was across to the next branch. It was slippery, but he steadied himself.

Pitter-patter, pitter-patter.

CRACK! BOOM!

He wiped the rain from his face. Prepared for the next

move. Another deep breath. Another step.

The branch bowed beneath his weight. "Don't worry," he told the owl as he shimmied farther out. "We'll be all right."

SNAP!

A twig splintered under his heel and he grabbed the branch. Instinctively, he held on to the owl—and looked down. He hadn't meant to.

The twig dropped, disappeared into the darkness.

His heart hammered on his ribs like the rain on his head.

Pitter-patter, pitter-patter.

CRACK! BOOM!

"Once upon a time . . . Once upon a time."

He focused on the tree house. He was closer. Just a few more steps and he'd be at the thin branch. He wouldn't be able to stay there long. But from there, all he'd have to do was reach across to the other tree.

"Hooo."

He took another deep breath. A step. Step. Step, and his toes bent around the thin branch.

He was one tree away now. The thick branch under the tree house was just there. Right there.

He only had to reach.

Pitter-patter, pitter-patter.

CRACK! BOOM!

Keeping one hand over the owl, he stretched his leg toward the branch on the other tree. The gap was wider than it looked. Too big for him to step over. Too big for him to reach. And below, there was nothing. Just a long way down—then the cold, hard ground. And monsters patiently waiting.

Pitter-patter, pitter-patter.

CRACK! BOOM!

The thin branch below him creaked. It bent.

His body lurched downward. But he grabbed the trunk. He held on tight.

Pain seared within his arm, but he focused on the trunk and the branch. He couldn't fall.

"Trust me. Jump." The words came back to him—the words he had heard on the beach when the water had pulled him under. "Trust me. Jump!"

Yes, that was what he had to do. He had to jump.

Pitter-patter, pitter-patter.

CRACK! BOOM!

The boy pulled air deep into his lungs and bent his knees. *Just push off,* he told himself. *Just jump.*

But what if he didn't make it? What if he fell?

Pitter-patter, pitter-patter.

CRACK! BOOM!

The branch below him split. Tumbled away.

"Jump!" he shouted. But he couldn't. His feet wouldn't.

> He reached.

>> He stretched.

>>> He dropped . . .

RETURN

"AAAHHH!"

The boy fell and fell. Leaves whipped past him. Arms flailed to get hold of a branch, a trunk, anything. . . .

His back hit a lower limb. He cried out but grabbed it tight. *Breathe,* he told himself through the pain. *Breathe.*

Steady again, he peered under the blanket. The owl's bright eyes stared back at him.

"Hooo."

The boy nodded. "We'll be there soon."

Above, he could see the tree house. His fall had dropped him out of one tree and onto a lower branch of the next tree—the tree where the house sat quietly waiting for him.

Pitter-patter, pitter-patter.

CRACK! BOOM!

The lightning was closer. The thunder was louder.

He had to pull himself up. Fast.

Grimacing through the pain rippling up his arm, the boy climbed up toward the tree house. One branch, two, three. His feet scrambled over the thick bark.

Pitter-patter, pitter-patter.

CRACK! BOOM!

He squinted against the pounding rain.

One more branch. Just one more.

He pulled. And pulled. Higher and higher.

He scurried behind the wall of leaves and curled up on the wide planks of the tree-house floor.

Breathe. Breathe. Breathe.

The wind roared outside, and the raindrops plinked off the thick leaves above. The boy's heart began to calm as he felt the planks beneath him. He had done it. He had brought the owl over the trees, through the storm, to safety. He had protected them.

"We made it," he said, his face cracking into a thin smile as he peered at the owl under the blanket. "We're safe."

"Hooo." The owl blinked.

The boy leaned back against the tree's trunk and carefully pulled the edges of the blanket out of his waistband. He spread out the fabric, tucked his arms and legs inside, then pulled up a corner so his head was covered too. Curled up, with the owl warm against his belly, the boy rubbed the soft skin of his finger on his lip and told himself not to worry.

Sleep didn't capture the boy for a while, but finally the thunder stopped rolling and the lightning stopped flashing, and the boy's mind began to drift.

Until a brightness glowed in front of him. The tree house lit up, green leaves bathed in a yellowy white. Had daytime returned so quickly?

The light swept over him, and then it was gone. Darkness settled again.

His heart quickened. It wasn't daytime. It was the light! His parents' light! They were calling to him, searching for him. They hadn't left!

He stuck his head through the leaves and twisted around as far as he could, but the light had disappeared. Where had it gone? More importantly, where had it come from?

The boy thought back to when he had seen the light on the beach. It had returned a second time. Hopefully, it would return now, too. And when it did, he'd have to pay attention.

"Hooo." The owl shook itself out from under the blanket.

"It's okay," the boy said. "It'll be back. Watch."

He tapped on his knees. Then tapped on his thigh. Started to pull a loose thread from the edge of the blanket, but stopped himself and tried to put it back. He stared out into the darkness, wishing the light would . . . just . . . come . . . back. . . .

And it did. The light pulsed through the branches, illuminating each line of leaves in turn. It covered the boy with warmth.

"I'm here!" he shouted, waving his arms. "Stop!"

The light hovered over him for a second, and he wanted to hug it close. "Yes! You see me!" He waved harder, a hopeful smile budding on his face.

Then the light moved on.

The boy's arms dropped to his sides as he stared into darkness.

The light had left him again. It had missed him on the beach and it still couldn't see him high up in the trees.

"Nooo!" He punched the leafy wall of the tree house. "No. No. No!"

He gazed in the direction of the light, wishing he could punch something harder. Scream until the light came back. But his anger fizzled into despair. He knew the light wouldn't return. As much as he wanted to be protected, to be saved, he knew that if he was going to get home, he would have to get there himself.

"At least my parents are looking for me," he said,

trying to weave hope into his voice for himself as well as the owl. "They must be—"

But the owl was no longer beside him. "Owl? Owl?" The boy searched the tree house and the branches outside. Finally, he spotted a small brown owl flying high in the treetops.

"Owl," he whispered.

The hollowness inside him deepened.

His shoulders sagged, but one thing kept him buoyed: his parents were still searching; they hadn't given up. He curled his fingers around this thought and held on to it tight. This time as he burrowed under the blanket, he believed he wouldn't be alone for long.

Hope lifts, propels people forward.
But hope is often thin,
and disappointment kills it quickly.
The boy had had so much disappointment already.
And more would come.
But he did have resilience.
That kind of armor is gold.
I watched, and I waited.

MIRROR

MORNING HAD ARRIVED. THE STORM CLOUDS had cleared away, leaving a powder-blue sky without a single cloud. The color reminded the boy of something. He closed his eyes and tried to picture it. But all that came was a dome of blue.

"Whatever," the boy mumbled. He was tired of being betrayed by his own brain. Couldn't it give him one more nice memory? A memory where he could feel his parents' warmth. And care. And love.

Forget the memory. Soon he'd be with them in person. He'd be at the Umbrella Beach.

The boy pulled the blanket off his lap and felt for the sea grapes in his pocket. The piece of fabric was still there, but he had fewer sea grapes than before. Some must've escaped during his fall. Worry scratched at his gut, but he wasn't hungry. Not for them, anyway. He hoped he'd have his refrigerator soon.

Leaves around him were cupped with water left over from the storm, so he filled his belly. Then, holding the blanket high, he stretched, extending his foot across the wooden planks of the tree-house floor.

"That's not how you do it."

The boy halted. That wasn't the bully. And there was no one else in the tree. He glanced down. He couldn't see anyone below.

"Who's there?" he asked.

"You have to press hard, but be careful."

He didn't recognize the voice, but it sounded like a boy, like him. . . .

"Is this you?" The boy narrowed his eyes. The bully was probably making a joke. But the bully didn't reply. Instead another boy's voice said, "I know. I'm doing it."

This wasn't the bully's voice either. But it was in the boy's head, like the memory of his mother.

"Ouch!" said the second voice.

"I told you," said the first. "You have to do it slowly. See?"

"Yeah," the second replied, a smile in the word. "I can do it."

The boy felt something move under his feet and peered down. Lines were slicing into the wood, thin gutters being dug out as he watched. No, they weren't lines; they were words: *E + O's Hideout*. Others were already there: a shape like a sun, and a moon, and something else that looked like a spooky dog.

He rubbed his fingertips over the crevices and they felt comfortable, like he knew them. "I made these," he said. "I remember! At least, I know I carved the sun and moon. And I carved a sword, too, somewhere. . . ."

He stood up and there it was, right where he'd been sitting, a carving of a sword in the old wooden plank.

This was *his* tree house! From his home. But what was it doing in this forest? And who carved the words and the weird, scary dog? A friend? He must have a friend.

The boy's heart flew. He reached for the wooden boards . . . but they dissolved at his fingertips. He was left standing on a wide branch, curled within the wall of leaves. The tree house wasn't real. Had it been just a memory?

He stamped his foot. He had been so *sure* it was real. He had climbed over to it. It had kept him dry and safe. But he had been teased again.

Enough. The boy wanted his real tree house. He had to get home. He had to get to the Umbrella Beach.

Tucking the blanket under his arm, he scooted down from the tree and glanced around for the Wolf. He couldn't see it, or smell it, but he still stepped cautiously away from the trunk. Quickly he found the stick he'd left nearby the night before, then started to walk toward the light.

One step, two steps, three . . . He stopped. Which way had he come? Which way was he supposed to go? When he had run from the Wolf, he hadn't paid attention to his direction, and now he'd lost the path he was on the day before.

The light! He gazed up to where his tree house had been, but the branches were so thick, he couldn't tell which one he had been sitting on or from where the light had shone. And the trees peered down so close together that he couldn't see the sun. He couldn't tell which way was north or east. He couldn't tell which way was home.

"You should never have left. Someone might've seen you on the beach. A boat could've rescued you. But no one will see you here. In these trees. Hidden away. No one will ever find you."

The boy crumpled to the ground, a small heap on a large flat rock that rose up from the forest floor.

"But I was so sure I should come." The despair he'd been trying to hold back leaked into the boy's heart. "I saw my mother and the light; I spent the night in the tree house—my tree house! They were supposed to be signs, so why am I still no closer to home?"

A tear escaped from his eye and fell into a puddle by his knees. The storm had left tiny pools in the crevices of the rock, each one mirroring the tall trees looming all around him. And this one held something else. He leaned in closer.

Staring back at him was a pair of eyes. He blinked— and the eyes blinked too.

Below them was a mouth. He smiled shyly, and the mouth in the water did the same.

He brought his hands to his face, cupping each cheek. In the small pool, watery hands cupped watery cheeks.

It was *him*! He was seeing himself for the first time since . . . he couldn't remember.

He stared at his reflection. Curls sprouted out of the top of his oval face. A round nose floated below his eyes. Eyebrows hung like dark crescent moons.

"Hey," he said.

Hey, he imagined the mirror saying back. *Are you lost?*

He nodded, and the watery mirror did the same.

"I'm trying to find my parents, but I was chased and . . ."

The mirror stared back at him.

"Never mind. My name's— Oh, I don't know my name. What's yours?"

The mirror stayed silent.

"You don't know your name either?"

The boy and the mirror laughed together, all his fear and confusion rushing out in one big snort that was loud enough to disturb the birds in the trees. But the boy didn't care. At last he had a friend. A friend who understood.

He laughed so hard, he fell on his back clutching his side. He glanced at the puddle, but his friend had disappeared. He scrambled back up so he was over the puddle and smiled.

"There you are. Promise you won't go away again."

Tiny pieces of twigs had drifted into the puddle, forming small inverted Vs on either side of the mirror's head. It looked a bit like the owl, without the feathers.

The mirror smiled back as a shadow fell over them, and the boy's heart skipped. The Wolf? He whirled around, but it was only a cloud passing overhead.

"You'd better watch out," he told the mirror. "There's a beast here. A Wolf that goes like this."

He curved his hands into claws and twisted his mouth into a snarl.

"I got away from it. But"—the boy leaned closer to his reflection—"I don't know if I can again."

In the pool, his mirror frowned.

The boy gasped. He jumped back. A reflection wasn't supposed to be different. And it wasn't supposed to change.

The eyes. They were younger somehow. The cheeks smaller. The nose like a button.

"You're not me," the boy said. "Who are you?"

He stared. He squinted. He exhaled slowly.

"Are you . . . ? You're . . . You're my brother."

The boy searched his heart, and a warm feeling bubbled up inside him. "You're the other voice in the tree house. I was telling you to be careful. It was when we were making those pictures, wasn't it?"

He remembered. It was still fuzzy, but he could see the small shape of his brother in the tree house, both of them on their knees, using their matching red penknives to carve their drawings in the wood.

"Are you a memory, or are you real?"

His brother smiled but stayed silent.

"You wouldn't reply if you were a memory. You must be real, but I don't know how. Where are you? Are you with Mom and Dad?"

His brother nodded.

The boy sat back on his heels. "I wish you could tell me where home was. I wish I was with you."

Suddenly his brother's face turned sad.

"What's wrong?" The boy leaned forward again.

His brother looked so small, so sorrowful. He opened

his mouth like he wanted to say something, but no words came from the puddle.

"I wish you could tell me," the boy said, then, "Maybe you miss me."

The face nodded, and faded.

"No!" The boy reached out to protest, but it was too late. His brother was gone, replaced by the boy's own reflection.

Sadness filled him. Once again he'd found a friend, some comfort, only to be deserted. Abandoned. Alone.

And yet this time something had been left behind: a fact that the boy held close.

"I have a brother." His lips curved upward with the words. "I have a younger brother. And he misses me."

He stared into the empty puddle, but in his mind he could still see the face. His brother's face. Grinning back at him.

"I probably teach him all sorts of things," the boy said. "I help him, like I did with the carvings. Maybe I tell him stories. When I get home, I'm going to tell him all about this adventure."

"If you get home. You're lost, remember? Oh yeah, remembering isn't exactly a strength of yours." The bully laughed.

"Go . . . A . . . Way!" The boy sat up and slapped the

side of his head. "Ouch." Not a good idea.

He stood, retied the blanket around his neck, and picked up his stick.

"I'll keep walking until I find the way if I have to," he told the bully. "Anything will be better than sitting here listening to you. I have to get home. I have a brother who misses me."

The bully snorted. *"Go on then."*

The boy frowned. Slowly he turned in every direction, trying to see something familiar, something that looked like it pointed where he needed to go.

"Something . . . something . . . ," he whispered, willing his path to appear. "Come on, show me something."

But the forest looked the same in every direction. He gritted his teeth, curled his hands into angry fists, then . . .

A whisper tiptoed over the leaves.

"Come back. Come back."

It wasn't his father's voice or his mother's. It was the small voice from the tree house. It brought with it the throb in his head and something else. . . .

"Ollie?"

That was right! He could remember his brother's name. It had jumped out of his memory and onto his tongue.

"Hurry up and come back." This time the voice wasn't

in his head like a memory. It was in the air, all around him, like when he'd heard his mother and father before.

The throb in his head pulsed harder, harder, and the boy pressed the spot to send it away. It worked. The pain stopped.

"I'm coming!" he shouted, jumping into the air so his words could travel farther. "I'm coming." His words got quieter as his shoulders sagged. "At least I would, if I knew the way."

A brisk breeze spun past the boy, picking dried leaves off the ground and swirling them into the treetops. Branches bowed aside, clearing a path to the marshmallow clouds floating in the deep blue sky.

The leaves spiraled higher and higher, until they danced in front of the clouds.

The boy's mouth twitched as he watched the leaves parade across the sky, twisting and turning until they formed a shape he started to recognize. A round head, pointed ears, long wings, big round eyes.

"An owl!"

The wings flapped, then flapped again, and again. The leafy owl glided in a circle in the sky above the trees, then turned toward the boy. It raced down, down, down, and the boy ducked when it got near. But the owl swooped above his head and flew away into the forest. The treetops swayed and closed out the sky again, but where the owl had flown, dried leaves rained slowly to the ground, lit up by a sparkling ray of sun.

"The light!" The boy jumped, waving his stick in the air. "That's the direction of the light."

He ran on for Umbrella Beach.

UMBRELLA BEACH

THE BOY FOLLOWED THE RAIN OF LEAVES for what seemed like forever. When he grew hungry, he devoured the rest of his sea grapes, but when he was tired, he didn't stop. His feet ached from walking on the twigs. His skin stung in the hot air. His breath dragged out with each passing hour. But he felt sure he'd reach Umbrella Beach soon.

The thick treetops blocked out the sun, but he could tell it was moving across the sky. Rays pierced the gaps in the leaves in ever-lower angles, and too quickly the shadows of the trunks grew longer and darker on the ground.

Fear curled into the boy's stomach like a snake, but he willed each foot to continue. He kept his eyes on the path and held his stick high, in case the Wolf returned.

One step and the next, over rocks and twigs. One step and the next, through stinging branches. One step and the next, again and again.

Until the leaves stopped falling, the forest exhaled . . . and he was on the other side.

The boy blinked in the twilight, his heart blooming. He had made it. He was safe. He just had to find his parents.

The ocean sprawled out in front of him, a blue wilderness crawling with bigger waves than the ones he'd seen on the other side of the forest. Round claws tipped with a froth of white rolled toward him, then broke with a *SPLASH* against a coast of rocks. Big, flat rocks, crammed one after the other. Gray humps like stone giants bent over, heads down, showing their backs to the sky.

There was no white sand. No Umbrella Beach. No family. Nothing.

The boy had walked through the entire forest and found more of the same on the other side. Water and rocks, rocks and water.

The sky was on fire now, along with the boy's hopes. And the swelling ocean pressed in closer. He had come so far but was still alone and scared and empty.

"Told you."

"Shut up." The boy didn't want to hear from the bully now.

"Don't be a sore loser."

"Shut up!" The boy stamped his foot for punctuation.

"It's not my fault we came all this way. I told you to—"

"SHUUUUUT UUUUUUUUUP!" The boy raised his stick and banged it again and again and again against the rock at his feet. Anger crackled in every strike until the stick splintered into a thousand tiny pieces.

The boy stilled, stared at what he'd done. The remnants of his broken sword were scattered across the rock.

"No!" he cried, but it was too late. His stick was gone.

"That was smart."

Anger built within the boy again, a tidal wave threatening to crush him. He wanted to rage against the bully, this place, this useless quest. He wanted to break something bigger . . . something he didn't care about.

But then the light came.

"Hey!" the boy shouted, his anger dissipating into hope. "Over here. I'm here!"

He jumped up and down, waving his arms over his head. Could his parents see him? Was the source of the light close enough?

The light didn't linger. It pulsed over him, then out to sea. He was drowned in twilight again.

"No!" The boy kicked the pieces of stick at his feet. "No. No! NOOOOOOOOO!"

He couldn't let it leave him again. He was so close that he could feel it.

The light had come from his right, but that direction held only trees. Still he had to try.

He took off, running as fast as he could. He didn't think about the water. He didn't think about the Wolf. He just ran. Across the backs of the giants, jumping over the rivulets between the rocks. Around the crop of trees that jutted out of the Green Wall . . .

Then he stopped.

Dropping to his knees, the boy stared.

Ahead, a spit of land rose up against the water. Angry waves crashed around the base of the cliff, clawing to get higher.

On top loomed a giant pillar, a silhouette against the darkening sky.

A lighthouse.

And shining from under its crown was his parents' light.

Finding the path is only half the battle;
Staying the course requires strength.
Yet strength is rarely found,
and when found, even more rarely kept.
The boy had come far, but he still had much to overcome.
There was a chance for a good end to his story,
but chances are small and disappear quickly.
I sighed and I waited.

LIGHTHOUSE

A LIGHTHOUSE. OF COURSE! THAT WAS HOW his parents were sending out the light. That was how they had been searching for him, calling to him all along.

"Mom! Dad!" He waved as the ray pulsed over him. "I'm here. I made it!"

The light swept past him again, before disappearing across the ocean. The boy searched through the darkness for his parents coming to welcome him.

But no one was there.

"They're inside!" He pounded toward the lighthouse.

"You're going in there?" The bully sounded like he wanted to add *dummy. "It's dark. You won't be able to see."*

"There's the moonlight. And there'll be windows."

"Not many."

"Enough." But the boy slowed a little.

"You don't know what will be inside."

"Yes, I do. My parents."

"But what about the Wolf?"

The boy stopped. The lighthouse was close now, a giant soaring up in front of him.

He gulped. "The Wolf won't be there."

"You sure? I think I can hear it."

"No, you can't." The boy willed his feet to walk again. "It's my parents. And I'm not keeping them waiting any longer."

In the almost half-moon, the lighthouse became clearer with every step. It was gray, punched with rust-colored bruises and poked with thin, dark windows. The top was narrow and circled with a railing, like a crown. The base was wide, and it swelled into a rectangle on one side. A house! The keeper's house. Did his parents live there? Were they the lighthouse keepers?

The boy shook his head. No, that felt wrong. His parents were here for him.

He picked up his pace, ran to the side of the lighthouse. He stretched out his hand to touch it, hesitated, then let his fingertips graze its surface. It was cold, rough, worn.

He followed the pockmarked wall to a door on the far side of the house.

The boy's heart danced. He was finally going to see his

parents! After all this time, he had found them.

But what if they didn't like what they saw?

The thought slipped out so quickly and silently, it surprised him. Of *course* they would like him. They were his parents. His family.

"Once upon a time, there was a boy who was sure," he whispered.

The door's handle was coarse and raw, pitted where the salt in the sea air had made a meal out of the metal. Instinct told him to pull his hand back, but the boy's jaw set. Spreading the blanket cape around his shoulders, he pushed down.

"Mom! Dad!"

The door opened to a room large enough to take up most of the house. Thin streams of dirty moonlight came through two windows, one on each side of the space. It was barely enough to see by, but the boy could tell the room wasn't empty.

Stepping inside, he felt a wooden floor beneath his feet. As his eyes adjusted, he made out a cot under a window against one wall. Against the other wall sat a desk, a chair, and a bookcase. And along the back wall were a stove and what looked like an old-time refrigerator.

But his parents weren't there.

Cut into the back wall were two doors. One was closed. But the other was open.

He ran to the open door.

"Mom! Dad!"

It led to a bathroom: gray tiles, a grimy metal tub, a small sink hanging off the wall, and a toilet with a broken seat.

But no parents.

He turned the knob of the closed door. It must go to the lighthouse, he guessed. It was locked.

"Ollie!"

He banged. Hard. His forearms slammed against the wood. *Bang. Bang. Bang!*

He kicked the bottom of the door, and . . .

Click.

The lock gave way. A crack appeared between the door and the wall.

"Mom? Dad?" the boy whispered.

He cracked the door wider.

A stench of old air slammed into the boy, and he recoiled, quickly pinching his nose.

Inside, the lighthouse was darker than the keeper's house. There was only one window, a very small one, and it was covered in mud and grime. The little moonlight that fought through the dirt to get inside outlined a round, empty room with a staircase weaving up the far wall.

"Ollie?"

His voice sounded high, and he released his fingers from his nose.

His family must be at the top of the lighthouse, near the light. That was why they couldn't hear him.

"You have to be kidding!" the bully said.

"Be quiet."

"You don't know—"

"BE QUIET!" The words echoed across the wooden floor.

Pulling the edge of his cape around him, the boy grasped the railing. The stairs creaked. *Please don't break,* he prayed.

"Mom? Dad?"

He spiraled higher and higher, and the staircase grew tighter and darker. A small window gave him a patch of moonlight, but one more step and he was smothered in black again.

"Ollie?"

He leaped up the stairs two at a time and finally emerged in a small, round room flooded in yellowed moonlight from windows on every side. In the middle of the room sat a block of iron so tall and wide, the boy couldn't see around it. It looked like some kind of machine. Next to it, a ladder hung down from a hole in the ceiling.

"Are you in here?"

He ran around the machine, a strange-looking contraption covered with knobs and dials and handles. Green paint peeled off its surface, as though it were trying to escape the orange rust underneath.

But still no parents. No Ollie.

A shuffling noise came from above, and his heart leaped. "Mom! Dad!"

The boy ran to the ladder, slid his cape protectively over his back, and grabbed a rung. A flash in his head took him back to when the water had dragged him down, when he'd been in the pink tile place and heard the watery voice: *Trust me. Jump!*

"Go away," he whispered. He didn't have time for things he couldn't explain.

He pressed down on the rung, preparing for the pain in his arm, but it didn't come. The rung disintegrated. His palm was coated with dark orange crumbs.

"Don't fall apart now." *How did my family get up there?* he wondered. He grabbed a section of the side rail that was still metal and placed his foot on the first rung, near the outside where it looked strongest. He pushed off and exhaled. The rung supported his weight. He tried the next, and the next, hopping over rungs that looked too far gone. Finally he poked his head up through to the floor above.

"Ollie?"

There was more light in this room, but at first glance, he still couldn't see his family. The room was empty except for what looked like a large bowl in the middle.

He pulled himself completely up and gazed around. Nothing. Empty. But how could that be?

He paced the wooden floor; maybe there was a door or a hallway to another room. But all he found were floor-to-ceiling windows that looked out on the sand and grass below. There were no clouds around the moon now, and the boy had a clear view in all directions. Everything looked small—as small as he felt. He was high above a grass-covered cliff. To the south, trees draped over the edge. The clawlike waves pounced to the north and east. The Green Wall loomed large to the west. And from here, he could look over the tops of the trees, hundreds of them, an army of leafy warriors standing guard around the lonely lighthouse.

But the boy didn't want an army. He just wanted his parents.

He searched the room again.

"Mom?"

No answer.

"Dad?"

No answer.

"Ollie . . . ?"

He walked all the way around the big bowl. Checked every inch.

Then collapsed on the floor.

His family wasn't here. Had he arrived too late? Had he missed them?

Tears clouded his eyes as disappointment trampled his hope. His journey was supposed to be over. They were supposed to be here. So why was he still alone? He wrapped his arms around his belly, holding back the threatening sobs. He had been so sure his parents had sent the light to find him. The light had been his beacon, and he had followed it for—

The light.

A realization tugged on the boy's brain. He pushed himself up and stared inside the bowl again. It was large and round, with a hole in the bottom that housed wires and broken glass but looked like it was waiting to hold something else. Something big. In fact, this whole room should've held something big.

The boy's pulse quickened.

The lighthouse didn't have a bulb.

SHELTER

A CRY CAUGHT IN THE BOY'S THROAT. HE HAD *just* seen the light shining from the lighthouse, from this very room!

But how could that be if there was no bulb? Had someone taken it out? They couldn't have. He had raced to the lighthouse and come straight up here. He had come in by the only entrance.

He stepped back, staring out the window at the trees of the Green Wall lined up outside the lighthouse.

What kind of place made refrigerators appear out of thin air? Showed his brother in a puddle? Made a pathway from an owl of leaves? And lured him with a light that had no bulb?

His back tightened as fear began to blister in his stomach. Then a noise pricked up his ears. A noise he'd heard before.

"Hmm mmm hmmm mmm."

Joy extinguished the boy's worry as his mother's voice sang out again. It was louder now, echoing around the room.

And with it came the horrible pain in his head, pulsing, stabbing, attacking his brain.

He pressed his hands on his temples, tried to stifle it. He focused on the voice.

"*Hmm mmm mmm. . . .*"

"It's 'Here Comes the Sun.' It's Mom. Mom!" he shouted. "Where are you?"

"It's okay," she said, her voice sweet and light. "I'm here."

She was here! He had been right after all. His family did want him. They had sent the light . . . somehow. He just had to find them.

Bracing himself against the pain in his head, the boy ran back to the hole in the floor, down the ladder, and onto the stairs.

"*Hmmm mmm mmm hmm mmm mmm mmm.*"

"I'm coming," he shouted, then winced as his head throbbed again. "Go away," he told the pain, pressing on the spot. "I have to find my mom."

The pain obeyed, releasing him, and he dashed down the wooden stairs after his mother's voice. Turning, turning, turning around the wall as fast as his feet could carry him, until he came to the bottom and burst through the door into the keeper's house.

"Mom?"

Barely any light came through the windows now. Darkness had descended outside, leaving the room filled with shadows. The boy searched the house again, even looking under the cot, but he couldn't find his mother.

Sorrow bit at his heart, but he told it, "She's here. I heard her. She's here."

"Who says?"

"She's here!" The boy stomped his foot, then hurried to the only place he hadn't checked: outside.

Clouds had crowded in front of the moon above the lighthouse, and the wind whistled around it. On one side, the Green Wall was dark and tall, and on the other, waves crashed hard against the cliff.

But in between, the boy saw nothing but open space.

"MOM!" he shouted, not caring what heard him. "MOM! MOM! MOM!"

Silence.

His mother wasn't here. It must've been just another memory, tricking him. Taunting him.

Tears welled in his eyes, and he banged the side of his head. "Stop messing with me."

"Yeah, that's going to help."

"Be quiet."

"You're the one who should be quiet. Haven't you noticed where you are? Don't you know what could be behind you?"

Dark. Monsters. Beast. The boy had forgotten!

He whirled around, but he couldn't see the Wolf. The bully was baiting him. But just in case, he sprinted back to the keeper's house and slammed the door. It was thin and worn; the Wolf could easily blow it down. So he dragged the desk across the floor and pushed it up against the door. Better. He closed the door to the lighthouse, too, in case the beast had somehow crept inside, twisting the knob until it was locked again.

Then he collapsed on the cot. And his heart broke.

He had shelter now, a roof, but it wasn't his home. Couldn't be his home. The walls looked as though they might fall over if they weren't attached to the lighthouse. And the cot was rickety. A scrawny mattress lay in the frame, but it wasn't much of a buffer against the wooden slats holding it in place. A stained pillow sat on one side.

Was this it? Was this all he had? All he'd have forever?

He cradled his stomach, holding back the sadness that threatened to consume him. "Pretend you're somewhere else," he ordered himself. His eyes squeezed against the flood of tears behind them. He wouldn't cry. He couldn't give in. "Pretend you're home, with Mom and Dad, with Ollie."

He might never get there, but he had to at least hold on to his wish. Taking a deep breath, he puffed up the pillow as best he could, untied his cape from around his neck, and spread the blanket over him, curling his legs so he was covered from his toes to his nose.

Tomorrow would be better. Tomorrow he'd wake up and everything would be okay.

"Once upon a time, there was a boy who had a happy ending."

He hoped.

Hope drives people home—until they remember.
When they see the path they must follow,
fear takes over once more.
I couldn't shield the boy from it.
He had to see before he could let go.
He had the light, but he still needed direction.
I gave him a thread to unravel.
It wouldn't be long.
I watched, while I waited.

MAP

THAT NIGHT THE BOY'S DREAM WAS DIFFERENT. He wasn't alone in the ocean; he was in a boat, orange with dark blue edges and a thin mast sticking up from the inside. A smooth wooden cradle surrounded by water. Around him, the ocean tensed. A bubble burst on the surface—a shriek escaped. Water surged beneath the boat, rising up the sides, invading the boy's safety. He tried to keep it out, but it flooded in around him.

Pulled on his arms.

Dragged him under.

Down into the darkness.

He awoke flailing, trying to stop his descent. But his arms and legs were caught.

"AAAAHHHH!"

He opened his eyes. He was inside a dome, light blue with stained patches. The boy thrashed, and it tightened around his face. He pulled his hand loose. Tugged the cover away.

The blanket. Of course. He hugged it to his chest. He

wasn't being attacked by monstrous waves. He was lying on the cot inside the lighthouse keeper's house, with all the danger locked outside.

He shuddered as he remembered his dream. Why wouldn't the water leave him alone? He shook his head, willing the image away, then sat up.

No wind howled outside. The boy tied the blanket back around his neck, then shoved the desk away from the door and cautiously crept through.

The day was just waking up. The sky was a dusty gray, punctured by a bright red sun. The Green Wall was still dark, the lighthouse a silhouette. Beyond the cliff, the ocean stretched lazily toward the horizon, which was piled with dark clouds.

Everything looked empty. Alone.

Just like him.

He had found the light, and it had brought him nothing. No parents. No family.

In fact . . . yes. The boy frowned. It had been one, two, three days since he had been born on the beach and he hadn't seen another soul. He had traveled across the sand and through the Green Wall and not seen one other person. The birds and the Wolf didn't count. Not one other person like him.

He really was alone.

The boy tramped back into the house. Closing the door behind him, he slumped onto the cot.

What could he do now?

"Nothing. You're lost. Completely lost."

"But I can't give up. I can't just stay here."

"You can't do anything else. You're not smart enough or brave enough or . . ."

The bully's voice droned on, but the boy tuned it out. Was the bully right? Would this have to be his home now?

He couldn't let that happen. His brother missed him, needed him. He'd called the boy home, sent the owl to guide him here. The boy had to find out why.

Maybe something in the keeper's house would help him find his parents. It was only a sliver of hope, but the boy grasped onto it tightly.

"You're more of a butthead than I thought."

"I'm not a butthead."

"You are if you think there's anything useful in here."

"Maybe something was left for the next lighthouse keeper."

"A broken lighthouse doesn't need a keeper."

The boy pressed his lips together but straightened against the bully's words.

The room didn't look much different now than it had the night before. Only a few of the sun's rays were able to push past the grime on the glass.

Yet, in the morning light, the boy could see one new thing: in the center of the floor was a rectangle where the wood was darker. A rug must have been there. How funny to think that this used to be someone's home. The keeper had read books from that bookcase. Cooked on that stove. Worked at that desk.

But now it was all empty, abandoned. The boy couldn't see how anything in the house would help him, but he had to look. He couldn't let go of his hope.

Dropping to his knees, he peered under the cot. Just dust and mouse droppings. He searched in the kitchen area, but there were only two metal shelves in the stove, and the refrigerator was bare. He put his head into the bathroom and quickly pulled it out again. Nothing in there would help him.

He flopped back onto the cot and frowned. He had looked everywhere but found nothing. Was there somewhere he was missing?

Outside, the sun blinked. A ray threaded through the web of grime on the window and into the house. It swung across the room, floor, bookcase—and landed on the desk.

The boy's eyes followed, his heart beating faster. Was this the lighthouse again? No, that beam was bigger and it couldn't curve down to reach in here. But this ray did seem to have a purpose.

He strode to the desk, rubbing his fingers over its scarred grain. Maybe something was carved into its top like the pictures in the tree house. No. No clue there.

The boy scowled, then gazed more closely at the sun's ray. It didn't end on the top of the desk. It pointed to the middle of the front panel. To a hole . . . like for a drawer pull or a key.

He scrambled under the desk. Yes, a drawer extended back. He hadn't noticed it before, but there it was. And who knew what it was hiding.

Pulling up the chair, the boy sat and tried to grip the outside of the drawer with his fingertips. But it was too flush with the rest of the front panel to get a good hold.

He slid onto the floor. Reaching up, he banged on the back of the drawer with his fist.

"Come on. Open!"

It didn't budge. He had to get more momentum.

He scooted farther under the desk, then pressed his palms against the wood on its far side. The pain shot up his arm, but it didn't hurt the boy as much now. Maybe he was stronger. Grinning, he pushed up hard. The desk was heavy, but with a grunt, he tipped it over so its front was against the floor. He had a clear shot at the drawer now. Aiming carefully, he kicked the back of the drawer. Once. Twice. Three times.

CRACK!

The wood splintered. A piece broke off, and something white peeked out from inside.

The boy fished it out. A ball of yarn. The drawer held more items, but they had fallen down near the front. He dipped his hand inside but couldn't reach them. He frowned, then pushed against the back of the desk so it fell upside down on the floor, its legs sticking up toward the ceiling.

The rest of the drawer's contents spilled out on the underside of the desk: a pencil that looked as though it had been sharpened with a knife, a worn piece of eraser, a bobby pin, and a piece of paper, folded into uneven quarters.

Paper! Perhaps it held a message. The boy flattened out the paper on the floor.

It showed a map of a series of islands. There was one big, long island, or was it three islands strung together in a line? Smaller islands dotted the coasts of the bigger ones.

Two medium-size islands flanked the top and bottom of the line, and tiny specks of land were tossed around the ocean to the west and south.

One of the western specks was circled in black ink, and above the circle were two words: *Duppy Island.*

A black line had been drawn from the easternmost point of the speck out into the open sea. Next to it was the word *Lighthouse.*

"This must be where I am." The boy sat back on his heels. "I'm on Duppy Island."

He crumpled onto his back on the floor.

An island. He was on an island—and a tiny island at that. Nothing more than a speck in the ocean.

That explained why he hadn't seen another person since he had woken up on the beach.

"You know what that means, don't you?"

"I'm really alone."

"That's right! YOU'RE ALL ALONE. And there's no one to help you."

The boy shook his head. "No. I just have to get to the big island."

"Oh, sure. You just have to get to the big island. Have you even seen another island?"

"No, but . . ."

"No. That's right."

"It doesn't mean they're not there." He scrambled back up onto his knees. "Look, if this map is right, the beach would be here." He pointed to a southwest spot on the speck. "And the rocks would be here." On the north side. "There aren't any islands close to those parts. The closest island is—"

The boy clambered to his feet and ran out the door.

"What? Where are you going?"

He ran past the lighthouse to the edge of the cliff.

The horizon was still clouded with haze. He squinted and waved his hands at the fog hovering over the ocean. "Move!" he called out, wishing he could scoop the clouds away. They looked like they'd made a home in that spot, and impatience got the better of the boy. "MOVE!" he shouted again.

This time the sky cleared.

The boy's eyes widened and he let out a surprised yip. "How—" But his words froze when he saw what was beyond.

The steady line of the horizon was broken. Sitting in the middle was a gray hill rising up from the surface of the ocean. *Land.* Another island. It didn't look big, but that was probably because it was far away. It didn't matter.

People might be there—people who could help him get home.

"All right, smarty-pants. How do you plan to get there? You see what you have to go over first?"

The boy gulped. The surface of the ocean rose and fell before him, like the monster below was breathing . . . waiting . . .

"Are you going to swim? Ha ha ha ha ha."

The boy flopped onto his butt. He had run away from the beast, found shelter from the storm, but to get to the other island, he would have to go through the water.

With its fingers . . .

With its waves . . .

Ready to drag him down.

"That's what I thought. You're too scared."

But the boy didn't reply. He had other things on his mind. Images from his dream of the night before. Smooth wood. Orange, with dark blue edges. A thin mast waiting for a sail.

"I won't have to swim," he said.

"Why's that?"

"I'll go on a boat."

FOUND

A BOAT. WHERE COULD HE FIND A BOAT?

The boy had walked over most of the island, and he hadn't seen any boats. But there must be one somewhere. His dream had told him so. Hadn't it?

The lighthouse keeper probably had a boat. Where would it be? Not in the lighthouse. The boy would have seen it.

He ran to the edge of the cliff. The water was calmer now, but there was no boat. He followed the coast south, the only part he hadn't explored yet. A small crop of trees sat at the edge of the cliff, and behind them, the land curved back toward the Green Wall. But it wasn't just a curve. The boy gazed out farther and could see that he was on one side of a gorge. It looked as though a giant had carved out a handful of earth from the edge of the island, and at the bottom was left a tiny gravel beach. Water crept up to it, then back, to and fro. On his hands and knees, the boy peered all around the gorge, but it didn't store a boat.

Gritting his teeth, he trod back toward the lighthouse. Did the keeper hide his boat? Where?

Something red by the trunk of one of the trees caught the boy's eye. He reached through the branches and pulled out a squashed Coke can. Crumpled next to it was an empty potato chip bag. Someone else had been here.

More trash was close to the lighthouse. A bottle of Sprite. A ripped Kit Kat packet. A ball of aluminum foil with what looked like green fur. Another chips bag: Nacho Cheese Doritos. He peered inside. Empty too.

The thought of food made his stomach grumble. But he'd eaten all his sea grapes. He wasn't supposed to need them anymore. He was supposed to be with his family already. "Arrrrgghh!"

The boy unraveled an edge from the ball of foil. A tiny insect poked its head out and scurried onto the boy's finger. He shook it violently. *Eww.*

"Stupid trash." He threw the foil. It landed a few feet from the Green Wall and then rolled into the darkness.

Into the trees.

The boy narrowed his eyes, and a bud of a memory sprouted. Yes, he remembered! He'd read a book where someone built a raft . . . *Robinson Crusoe!* The boy smiled.

If it worked for them, maybe it could work for him. He could make a raft out of logs and finally get off this island and go home and have all the food he wanted.

He strode up to the Green Wall—and fear poked him in the stomach. The last time he had seen the Wolf was in the forest. That was a while ago, but the beast had followed him from the beach. It might have followed him here, too.

The boy stepped back. The trees stretched into the sky above him.

"This is a bad idea."

The bully might be right. He might be devoured by the beast. But a raft was his only chance. "I don't care what you think."

"Oh, you care. You know you do."

The boy squeezed his eyes shut. "Once upon a time—"

"That's not going to protect you."

"I said, I don't care what you think."

"I'm just saying, you'll need more than a story if you have to fight that Wolf. And that blanket over your back doesn't make you a knight."

The boy stomped his foot. "ENOUGH!"

He lifted his head high, crossed his arms, and stared into the Green Wall. The bully wasn't right, couldn't be right, because to succeed in this plan, the boy had to be the greatest knight that ever lived.

"Once upon a time, there was a boy who was invincible," he whispered, breathing in deeply and filling his lungs with knight superpowers.

He straightened his back, his blanket flapping behind him. "I'm coming in!" he shouted. "You know what I want, and you'd better give to it me."

Then he strode into the forest.

Even though he was far away from where he had first walked through the Green Wall, the forest here looked the same. Tall, thick tree trunks rose out of the earth like hairs from a giant head. Branches pointed in all directions, covered with leaves in every shade of green.

And, of course, there were the eyes. Flashing. Gawking. Watching him. None were the green of the Wolf's eyes, so the boy relaxed—a little.

He needed four or five sturdy branches, long enough that, sitting in the middle, he'd be out of the sea's reach. A few steps in, he spotted one that would be perfect. It was on a tree that was a short run from the safety of the clearing, and it sprang out from the trunk only a little higher than the boy's head.

"I can do this." The words slipped out of his mouth and swelled his heart.

He dashed to the branch and reached up. Wrapping his arms around the limb, he pulled down with all his might, but it didn't move. The boy lifted his feet off the ground so he was hanging from the branch, but it still wouldn't budge.

"*That's not going to work*," the bully said.

"Shut up." He climbed onto the stubborn limb, bent his knees, and jumped—but not too high.

"*You're going to have to do bet*—" the bully began.

"I said . . ." The boy's face grew hot, but he breathed in deeply. "I don't have time for you."

He bent his knees and jumped again, higher this time. But still the branch didn't break. It didn't even crack. Again, and again, the boy jumped on the limb, but nothing would snap it. Finally the boy jumped as high as he could, but when he came down, his foot landed wrong, and he fell to the ground with a *thump*.

"OWW!" He had fallen on his bad arm. The burning pain sprinted into his chest. Carefully, he sat up and examined the skin. A line of blood bubbled up between his wrist and his elbow where his arm had scraped the tree on his way down. He picked some leaves off the ground and pressed them against the cut. They stopped the bleeding, but not the hurt.

"Baby. It's just a scratch."

"Leave me alone."

The boy felt tears behind his eyes, but he shut them out. It wasn't just a scratch. It was a gash. But it didn't matter. He had to keep going. He had to make his raft so he could get home.

He stared at the branch again, narrowing his eyes as though they were powerful lasers cutting it down. But the limb stayed still.

"That's seriously the most brainless thing you've done yet." The bully laughed.

"I said, LEAVE ME ALONE!"

The boy trod farther into the forest in search of another branch. Plenty looked perfect, but they were all attached to trees. He climbed onto a higher branch that looked thinner, told himself not to be afraid, then held on to the trunk and jumped on it. The branch stayed where it was.

"This isn't going to work," he whispered, despair creeping up from his toes.

"I've been telling you that all along."

A crater formed in the boy's stomach, and he clamped his arms around his belly.

He just wanted to get home, to be with his family. He wanted to help his brother. Hug his mother. And, more than anything, he wanted to show his father . . . what? He hoped he'd remember when he saw him.

His father could probably build a raft. What would he think of the boy if he couldn't even make a boat?

He pounded his fist against the trunk of the tree, over and over. "Why can't I do this? Why? Why?" Then stopped.

He'd heard something below.

A creak . . .

a Crack . . .

a SNAP . . . then GGGRRRRRR!

The boy's heart halted. The Wolf! Had it found him? Holding his breath, he looked down.

THUD.

Leaves shook on the forest floor.

THUD.

Birds flew away.

THUD!

A mass of black and gray hair loped below him. Each

step made the boy's tree shudder. He held on tighter, tighter, digging his fingertips into the rough bark.

"Please . . . please . . . please," he whispered, willing the beast to pass by.

But the Wolf stopped, its nose twitching in the air.

The boy froze, not even daring to breathe. The only part of him that moved was inside, where his nerves churned like a tornado.

Outside, the wind picked up too. A gust screamed through the forest, bowing the trees from side to side.

The boy hugged the trunk, but the wind yanked at his arms, wrenched at his legs. He started to slip and screamed, "AAAHHHHHH!"

The Wolf's giant head twisted up, its mouth pulled back in a sneer, its yellow teeth glinting with drool. It stepped back, then rammed the bottom of the tree with its shoulder. The tree shook. The Wolf pounded, pounded, pounded. The trunk quaked.

The wind pushed harder.

And the boy lost his grip.

"Once upon a time," he cried, as he tumbled from branch to branch, "there was a boy who escaped."

A blast of wind drove around the trunk. It pushed under the boy, thrusting him into the air. He flew, flew,

flew, until he came back down to the ground away from the Wolf, closer to the clearing.

"Whoa!" he said, standing quickly and rubbing his arm. He glanced around for the horrible beast.

It was there, behind him, still at the base of the tree. And it hadn't seen him.

"I got free?" The boy grinned. "I got free."

But the Wolf's nose was sniffing. It turned. Its eyes narrowed on the boy's. It ROOOOAAARRRRRRED— then ran toward him.

Fear sprang up inside him.

"Once upon a time, there was a boy who was faster than the wind," he yelled as he sprinted through the trees. The lighthouse rose up ahead on the other side of the trunks. He pumped his arms and legs and repeated, "Once upon a time . . . once upon a time . . . once upon a time . . ."

He didn't stop when he broke through to the clearing. He didn't stop when he got to the lighthouse. He didn't stop until he was in the keeper's house, behind the door, with the upside-down desk safely blocking the entrance.

Only then did he breathe.

The boy curled on top of the cot, pulled the blanket

around himself, and rubbed the soft fabric on his lip.

"We're safe," he told the blanket. "We're safe."

But he knew it was a lie. He'd never be safe on this island, not with the beast.

BROTHER

THE BOY HAD TO ESCAPE. HE HAD TO FIND some way off this island. Or he was going to die.

Jumping off the cot, he swept up the map and circled Duppy Island with his finger. "I'm here," he said. Then he traced a line from there to the nearest island, straight across from the lighthouse. "That must be the one I can see." He measured the distance with his fingertip and thumb. So near.

But with all that water in between, it was so far.

Blackness. Dragging. Tugging. Waves pulling him—

down.

Down.

Down.

Too far.

He couldn't swim across that ocean. The monster under the sea was waiting. It was ready. It wanted to take him under.

A groan came from deep in the boy's throat. Maybe the bully had been right all along.

"I can't do it. I can't. I CAN'T!"

He scrunched up the map. Threw the wad as hard as he could. It bounced off the back wall and into the bathroom.

"You don't have to go. You can stay right here. In this house. In this shelter."

The boy sighed. He *was* safe here. But for how long?

"The Wolf will find me one day."

"Not if you stay inside and keep the door locked."

"But I'll need food."

"Sheesh, you're so demanding. Fine, go out, get more of those sea grapes, then lock the door and stay in here."

The boy didn't like the bully's solution. It dragged his shoulders lower and lower. But every time he thought about the inches on the map between the lighthouse and the bigger island—the inches that were miles and miles of open, hungry water—his stomach turned over.

He couldn't do it. He couldn't go across the ocean.

But he also knew that the bully was wrong. He wouldn't be safe in the house. Not for long. The Wolf would find him. And he wouldn't escape next time.

He was stuck. He'd never get home.

A thickness clogged his throat. Tears welled in his eyes. He closed them, but the drops still tumbled over his cheek.

"It'll be okay. Don't worry."

The voice . . . it was his own, but he hadn't said the words. They had risen up in his head, like before when he'd seen his memories.

His eyes snapped open. The boy sat up.

The thin mattress had puffed up below him. It wasn't a dreary stained white anymore; now it was covered with a cozy, navy-blue comforter and pillows decorated with hundreds of bright yellow stars. Around him, the cot unfolded into bunk beds, with black pipes supporting the bed above his head.

A thick gray carpet rolled across the wooden floor. Toys were scattered around it: a ball, a stuffed dragon, a book opened to colorful pictures of wizards and knights. A chest with HP etched on the top rested against the wall.

And the desk, standing right way up now, wasn't nicked and scratched. Instead the surface was covered with a glossy black sheen. Shelves unfolded up the wall behind it, packed with books and games. A computer sat on the desk, with a school of bubble-breathing fish swimming across the screen.

And the rickety wooden desk chair had bulged into a high-backed roller with a thick cushion on the seat. A green backpack with a bright yellow *E* embroidered on the pocket hung off the back of the chair.

The boy wasn't in the lighthouse keeper's house anymore. He grinned. This was *his* bed, *his* desk, *his* bedroom. In *his* home.

But how did he get here? Was it real?

He rubbed the soft material of his comforter. It felt real, but he'd been fooled before by the refrigerator and the tree house. He didn't want to hope too much, even though he couldn't help it.

"I'll protect you, okay? You don't have to worry."

It was his voice again, but not coming out of his mouth. The boy followed the sound and saw two boys sitting in the corner of the room, partly hidden by a red beanbag chair. *It's me,* the boy realized. *And Ollie.*

"I don't like the wolf," Ollie said. Tears lined his voice.

"Remember what I told you?" the boy in the beanbag chair said. "The wolf wasn't always a wolf. He was once a great king. . . ."

Ollie laid his head on his brother's shoulder. The boy lay on his own bed, watching himself tell the story. . . .

"The king was always happy, and everyone in his kingdom loved him. But he had a secret. When he was a baby, he had been cursed by a horrible witch. She didn't like the baby king's parents, so she cursed the king to turn into a scary wolf so everyone would hate him. But there was a second part to the curse. . . ."

Ollie sat up, gazing at his brother.

The boy leaned in to hear more.

"The witch's curse said that even though the king had to live as a scary wolf that everyone hated, he couldn't bite anyone, ever."

"And what about the prince?" Ollie asked.

The beanbag boy hugged Ollie closer. "The prince made a sword out of the best silver in the land, and he promised to slay the wolf if it ever got its bite back."

"Spit swear?" Ollie asked.

"Spit swear."

On the bed, a tear seeped into the boy's eye as he watched himself and his brother. He blinked.

And his bedroom was gone.

He was back in the keeper's house. With its dim light, overturned desk, and thin cot.

"NO! Come back!"

He closed his eyes, rubbed them hard, and prayed that when he opened them, it would be as though he had stepped through a window into that other life, his proper life.

But when he lifted his eyes, he still saw the faded wooden floor.

"Come back," he whispered again, remembering when

he'd heard his brother say those words in the air. "Come back."

"*It's not coming back.*"

"No." The boy gritted his teeth, hoping he could make the bully understand. "I know why my brother said that before, why he needs me."

"*Enlighten me.*"

"He has a wolf there, too," the boy said, narrowing his eyes. "And I have to help him."

"*Help him? You? You can't even help yourself.*"

The boy crossed his arms. "I got away from the Wolf twice."

"*Barely. You won't be so lucky next time. And you know it.*"

The boy didn't answer. He did know it.

"*It doesn't matter anyway.*"

"Why?"

"*To help your brother, you've got to get past something way more scary than that Wolf.*"

The water. The ocean. The monster lurking beneath the surface . . .

        waiting . . .

             watching . . .

                   hungry . . .

"*You'll never get past that . . .*"

"ARRRRGGGGGGH!" Anger exploded in the boy.

Why did he have to be so weak and afraid? Why couldn't he be brave and smart and strong? He threw the pillow across the room. Pulled the mattress up from its slats. Kicked the leg of the desk.

And it broke.

The old wood splintered, and the broken piece clattered onto the floor. A jagged stump was all that was left.

The boy stopped, his heart slowing. His eyes ran over the base of the desk lying flat on the floor, three legs and a stump sticking up. Around the base was a lip that was at least five inches tall. There were two breaks in the lip at the face of the drawer, but he could plug them, jam leaves in the tiniest gaps to make it waterproof.

An upside-down desk that could be so much more. It could be the help he needed. It could be his way home.

It could be a boat.

BOAT

THE DESK COULD BE HIS ESCAPE!

It would be like a raft, but better. The desk was wood, just like logs, so it should—it *would*—float perfectly. The broken leg could be the paddle, and he could break off another for the rudder.

A rudder. That's right! The boy could picture it. A perfect memory of a rudder, protruding from the back of a boat, carving a curvy path through the water.

The boy grinned.

And what about a sail? He could picture that, too. Big and white, billowing from a mast in the center of the boat. Like in his dream.

But where would he find a mast and a sail? Unless . . .

The boy untied the blanket from around his neck and ballooned it out in front of him. It wouldn't make a big sail, and it wasn't really the right material. But it could work. Instead of tying the blanket to one mast, he could attach it between the two legs on the back.

A boat. With a rudder, a sail, and a paddle. He'd be

across the ocean and on that other island in no time. He'd be home soon.

"You're not going to make it. You've got shelter here. You should stay."

"I can't stay here. The Wolf will come after me. It won't stop until it finds me. Besides, this isn't where I belong. I need to go home to my family. I need to help my brother."

"Pah! They haven't even come to find you. Who needs them?"

The boy gazed around the keeper's house that had shown him his bedroom and his brother. "I do."

He nodded firmly. He was going to escape, just like the Little Prince. He was going to sail to the other island, find his family, and live happily ever after—the same as in all the best stories.

He pounced on the desk and kicked the leg opposite the already broken one. Once. Twice. It was stronger than the other leg. "Come on!" he shouted, kicking harder. The leg snapped off.

"Good."

The jagged edges of the stumps were sharp, and the boy didn't want to get splinters while he was on the boat. Holding one leg up with his good arm, he hammered it onto the stumps. They didn't get quite smooth but close enough.

The broken legs had to be smooth too, so they wouldn't hurt his hands when he used them as his rudder and paddle. He raised one above his head and slammed the spiky end onto the floor.

It went straight through, smashing a hole in the wooden planks.

"Oops!"

The boy ran outside and, keeping an eye out for the Wolf, banged the sharp edges of the legs on the gravelly ground until they were no longer jagged. Back inside, he put one leg on the floor to use for the paddle and balanced the other one for the rudder between the two legs that would make the mast. He had to attach it, but how?

The boy sat back on his heels. What he needed was some kind of string or—the yarn in the drawer!

"Where did I put it?"

He peered around the desk. Not there. Had it rolled behind the stove? No. Refrigerator? No.

"There!" Under the cot.

If he wrapped the yarn around the rudder and around the bases of the two masts, it should stay in place well enough. He unraveled the yarn. There was plenty to attach the rudder and the sail, but first he had to cut it. He looked around for something to cut it with. No scissors. No knife.

The boy pursed his lips. He bit down on the yarn, but it didn't break. He stretched it, but that didn't work either. He rubbed it against the leg stumps left on the desk. They were too dull now.

"Rocks."

He ran outside again. Scouring the ground, he found the perfect stone: small and round so he could hold it but with one sharp point for cutting. Back inside, he scored the yarn with the stone. After four tries, he cut it.

"Yes!"

He wound the yarn around the rudder twice, three times. Then he held up the string so the rudder hung down like a pendulum. He shook it. The rudder slipped.

"Hmmm."

He did it again, keeping the thickest part of the rudder above the yarn and making the knot tighter. When he held it up this time, the rudder shimmied but stayed in place.

The boy grinned.

Keeping the rudder between the two masts, he tied the ends of the yarn to the bases. Good and taut. "You can hang down into the water and keep me on course," he told the former desk leg. "What next?"

Just the sail.

He picked up the blanket, his cape—his knight cape. It

was so soft. He touched it to his lips and his heart tugged. What if the blanket was ruined? But if it meant he'd get home faster, he had to use it. He'd just have to be careful.

"Don't be afraid," he told the blanket. "I'll be with you the whole time."

Carefully, he spread the blanket on the floor between the two masts. He cut the rest of the yarn into four pieces, then pressed one corner of the blanket to the bottom of a mast and wrapped it tight. He nodded. "Good." Soon he had every corner of the blanket tied up, in double knots to be sure it wouldn't blow away.

He stood up and stared at what used to be the desk.

Now it was a boat. *His* boat.

His lips curved into a smile that spread across his face.

"I made a boat."

ESCAPE

ALL THAT WAS LEFT WAS TO GET HIS BOAT safely to the water, then he could go home.

Sunlight crept through the windows, giving the room a warm glow. The boy squinted at the walls and noticed they had a pattern on them. He stepped closer. Flowers. Faded yellow flowers with light green stems that blended into the cracks of the wallpaper. They gave him a slight smile.

His fingers grazed over the pillow. The cold stove. The heavy bookcase.

His heart turned over. He was finally going to leave this island and the horrible beast. No more wishing. He had his escape.

But sadness wormed a hole in his excitement. This room had shown him his bedroom and his brother. It had been his home for a short time. In a strange way, he would miss it.

The ocean was calm. No wind. Perfect conditions for a ride on a boat.

Heaving and puffing, he had dragged his boat back the way he had come the day before until it touched the ocean.

The boy stuffed leaves into the holes by the drawer. Not many would fit. The drawer was in there tight. Hopefully it was watertight.

Now, this was it. His moment of escape.

All he had to do was push a little farther, so the boat floated on the tide. All he had to do was jump onboard and he could sail away. All he had to do was jump.

His stomach burbled like a volcano, ready to erupt. Wind whistled through the trees behind him and raked over the ocean in front. As the boat touched the surface, the water swelled far out near the horizon. The once passive waves grew quickly and turned toward the boy.

"Go away," the boy whispered, to the fear in his stomach as well as the monster out at sea. This boat would protect him. It would get him home. He had nothing to worry about anymore.

He waded into the warm water, slipping on the seaweed-covered rocks. He pushed his boat forward one inch, two, three, until the surface lapped the boy's knees and the boat bobbed in the trembling water. He held it tight, kept it steady.

"You know what you're doing?"

"Yep." He nodded. "I jump in, paddle out, then push the rudder away from me. The boat will sail around the cliff where the lighthouse is, then on to the other island." He paused. "No problem."

He tried not to think about whether he believed it.

"You really think it'll get you across?"

"Of course it will."

"You really think it'll stay afloat?"

"Sure . . . It will."

"You really think it'll keep you safe?"

"Yeah . . . It—it will?"

The boy swallowed. He couldn't hide his nervousness.

There was a chance that he was terribly wrong, that the desk wouldn't get him across. A wave could splash over the sides and sink him. Just like in his dream.

He closed his eyes and pictured himself on the boat, sailing across the ocean. The other island within his grasp. His parents and Ollie waving to him from the shore.

But the water rose, slapping the sides of the boat— pushing him off course. Pushing the boat over.

Blackness. Silence. Dragging him

> down . . .

> > down . . .

> > > down . . .

"No!" He tried to shove away the image, to keep his mind on his family, on his brother.

But he remembered the water on the beach trying to wrench him away from the shore. The waves by the boulder grasping at him. He felt the water on his legs now. Pulling. Yanking. Tugging.

He searched the ocean for the monster. It was still hiding beneath the surface, but the waves in the distance grew fatter, clawing their way to the coast. To him.

A rush of sea forced him backward. The wave grabbed his waist, reached for his neck. Surged into his mouth.

He fell, gasped, spluttered, holding the boat tighter.

He blinked away the drops and for a moment, the ocean disappeared. He was back surrounded by pink tiles, his hand no longer on the boat but on a metal ladder.

"Trust me. Jump!" he heard the watery voice shout.

"I'm trying," he cried, and pushed himself up. He was again standing on the flat rocks at the edge of the sea with his boat.

Another wave rolled toward him.

"No," he pleaded, and the wave retreated.

But it hurried back. It always came back.

A brick formed in the boy's chest.

He tried to calm his breathing. *Slow, heart. Slow.* "Once upon a time, there was a boy . . . there was a boy . . . there was a boy who conquered the seas?"

But the story wasn't working. His fear gripped him too tightly.

CLAP!

Black clouds billowed above him. Lightning shot down to the ocean.

The boy told himself to jump onto the boat.

He willed his body to move.

Wind roared louder around his ears. Waves crashed harder beside him. Water tugged and tugged and tugged.

Tears welled in his eyes. "No crying," he scolded himself. He needed courage. He needed to be brave. To be the knight.

"I am the knight," he said loudly, then whispered, "Please be the knight."

But the tears leaked onto his cheeks and clouded his eyes. "Go away," he told them. He couldn't let them get in his way. He had to get into the boat. He had to find his courage.

He lifted his hands to wipe away his fear . . .

And the boat sailed on without him.

Frozen in the warm ocean water, the boy watched his escape float away.

Fear is a prison and Doubt is the chains.
As long as the chains are strong, there is no escape.
The boy had come far, achieved much,
but he wouldn't be able to break his chains.
Yes, there would be only one end to his story.
I had to watch. I had to wait.

BIG BAD WOLF

CRUMPLED ON THE GRAVEL BELOW THE lighthouse, the boy rubbed his lip with his finger. But the softness didn't soothe his heart. The storm had dissipated fast, but it wasn't any solace. His sorrow had dug a chasm inside him and drained his tears. He didn't even have enough energy left to cry.

Why hadn't he climbed onto the boat? Why hadn't he swum out after it?

Because he was weak. A scaredy-cat. A chicken. That was why. He hadn't even *seen* the monster in the ocean, not actually, and its hunger still terrified him.

He had made a boat to sail past the monster—but hadn't trusted that he could.

He sniffed back the thickness in his throat and stared up at the lighthouse. It had been his last hope of finding his parents. His brother needed him, and he'd let Ollie down.

"Why'd you bring me here?" he shouted to the top of

the lighthouse. His despair flared into anger, and his hands closed into fists. "You gave me hope."

The lighthouse didn't reply. It just stared straight ahead, at nothing.

The boy shook his head and dug his toes into a patch of grass.

The lighthouse wasn't to blame; it was as lonely as he was. It had once been loved, been taken care of, and now it was abandoned and neglected too.

No, *he* was to blame. The bully had been right about him all along. The boy didn't want to believe it, but it *was* his fault he was alone.

And now he was going to stay alone.

His broken heart told him so.

"Don't you have anything to say?" he shouted to the bully. "Don't you want to tell me how brainless I am? What a coward I am? Come on. I know you're right."

But the bully was silent.

Anguish washed over the boy again. And this time, he sobbed. He didn't care about being strong anymore. He wasn't strong. He didn't even have his blanket. He had lost *everything*.

Except . . .

He reached into his pocket and felt the piece of fabric.

He still had that. But it couldn't help him.

The Wolf might as well come and eat him. He was too weak, too useless, too much of a waste. The Wolf should drill its glowing green eyes into him. Dig its claws into his flesh. Tear his loser legs and arms with its pointed teeth.

"You win," the boy whispered. "Come and scare me. Come and eat me. No one will care."

But the beast didn't come. Not even a leaf stirred in the trees.

"Even the Wolf doesn't want me," the boy said.

He collapsed on the ground, staring at the puffy white clouds drifting above him. None of them had stopped to help him. They saw him below—alone and scared—but they floated past. And when he needed them the most, they turned black and vicious.

Then a flash of brown swooped over him from the Green Wall. Flapping wings, pointy ears.

"Hoo."

The boy jumped up. The owl! It was the baby owl he'd rescued in the tree. It had followed him here. Maybe he did have a friend after all.

"Hoo."

The owl circled above him, then flew to the lighthouse

and perched on the railing at the top. Its big eyes looked down at the boy, but it didn't come closer. "Hoo," it said, like it was trying to tell the boy something. "Hoo. Hoo."

The boy fell onto his knees, his knuckles grating on the gravel. "I don't know what you want," he told the owl. "I can't help you anymore. I can't even help myself."

Maybe the bully was right. Maybe his parents hadn't looked for him. Maybe they didn't want him. Why should they, when he was nothing?

Just a small boy stuffed full of fear.

His mother had read him stories. His brother had made him laugh. And his father . . . he was supposed to show his father something. The boy had probably let him down. Just like he'd let himself down. He'd never show his father now, and his father would never love him.

He would never be good enough.

"RRRRRRROOOOOOOAAAAAAARRRRRRR!"

The boy trembled. Eyes wide, he curled himself around his knees and put his hands over his ears.

The Wolf!

It had come up behind him. He had called it. Dared it to eat him. And it had listened.

Stupid. Stupid. *Stupid.*

The ground shook with each of the Wolf's steps.

Closer.

Closer to the boy.

Closer to the boy's demise.

He shivered uncontrollably. Coiled tighter. As small as he could be. Squeezed his eyes shut.

Boom. Boom.

The beast stomped closer. Its hair grazed the boy's legs. Its breath seared the boy's skin. Its drool sizzled on the boy's cheek.

He felt a sharp sting. The tip of the Wolf's claw sliced into the boy's shoulder.

This was it.

This was the end.

STRANGERS

THE BOY WAS TRAPPED, HIS BREATH SHALLOW under the weight of the Wolf.

A shiver raced through him as he wrapped himself tight in his arms. His shoulder seared with pain where the Wolf's claw had ripped his skin. Every inch of him was ablaze with fear.

Around them wind raced. Thunder clapped. The ground shook, as the boy trembled.

A tear escaped his tightly shut eye and crawled down his cheek. He couldn't fight. He couldn't run. All he could do was hope the beast wouldn't strike.

"Hoo."

The owl! What if the beast attacked it? The boy couldn't let that happen. The Wolf lifted its head, but its attention didn't sway from the boy. Not even its nose twitched toward the baby bird. The Wolf leaned in closer, hot breath scorching the boy's head.

It was going to eat him.

"Hoo." Then turn on the bird.

"Stay away," the boy shouted, curling tighter. His heart screamed with terror as the beast's drool dripped on his shoulders. Terror for himself, but also for the owl. So small. It needed protection.

But the boy couldn't protect it now. He couldn't protect himself. He was going to die.

"Hoo."

No, the boy thought, as the Wolf's teeth got closer. *Stay away.* But the *hoo* sounded different this time. Lighter. Like it was tinged with a . . .

A mischievous giggle trilled in the boy's ear. It was his brother! And a sweet smell—his mother's perfume— wafted away the stench of the Wolf. His brother's laugh and his mother's perfume mixed together in the air around him, a song calling out to him. Reaching for his heart.

His head ached and his breath faltered, heavy in his chest. He had tried to get to them, to get home. But now he would never see them again. Never touch his mother's smiling face. Never see his brother's sparkling eyes. Never be able to help him.

His mother's voice came through the air: "You are my sun."

His brother's voice was light and pleading: "Come back."

The boy had thought the Wolf was what he wanted—what he deserved. He had called for this end to his story. But here was his mother again, and his brother, calling out to him. Still calling him home.

Was there a way . . . ?

The Wolf clawed a gash in the boy's leg—and he screamed.

"There's nothing you can do. The Wolf is too big. Too scary. It'll always win."

The boy's heartbeat quickened. And the ground quaked harder.

He thought of the story he had told his brother in the memory. The wolf in the story couldn't bite, but this Wolf could. He knew that from its stale breath.

He had told his brother the prince would slay the wolf when it got its bite back. How could he do that if he couldn't protect himself? He had made a promise to Ollie. What kind of brother would he be if he didn't do everything he could to keep it?

He didn't have a silver sword, and he wasn't a proper prince. But he had to slay this Wolf, or at least die trying.

"NOOOOOOOOOOOOOOOOOOOOOOOOOOO!"

The scream shot out of the boy as he felt the Wolf's thick drool on his face.

Opening his eyes, the boy stared into the dark tunnel of the Wolf's throat. Its gray tongue curled at the edges, a pathway inviting the boy inside.

"Once upon a time . . . there was a boy who was . . . STRONG!"

The Wolf's green eyes glared at the boy, piercing into his courage. But the boy gritted his teeth. He jammed his hands inside the beast's mouth and pushed on the roof. His forearms levered the jaws apart. His fingers scraped against the yellow fangs, but the boy didn't let go.

Around them, the wind died, the thunder stopped, and the ground settled. But the boy didn't notice. He focused on the Wolf. He concentrated all his strength on keeping the giant mouth open. The boy's arms ached with the effort, but he held them tight.

A slow growl rose up from the pit of the Wolf's stomach. Its breath blew against the boy's face, singeing his hair. It smelled of death.

"Hold on," the boy told himself. "Hold on!"

He willed all his energy into his arms. Ordered the pain to vanish. He pushed against the Wolf's jaws, keeping its monstrous mouth open.

The beast's growl grew louder.

The jaws pushed back.

"NOOOOOO! You will not get me. You will NOT get Ollie."

The boy groaned. He drove the Wolf's teeth back. And back. And back.

"Unnnhh." Harder. *Harder.* The boy pushed harder.

"It won't work. You can't beat it."

The Wolf's jaws bore down again on the boy, its mouth now covering his head, its teeth closing in around his ears.

"I have to," the boy said. "I *have to* beat it. I will."

Taking a deep breath, he heaved his body upward. Forced the beast's head away.

It screeched, stumbled backward.

The boy scurried out of the Wolf's reach.

"You can't hurt me!" he shouted. "I'm not afraid of you anymore."

The Wolf sat on its back legs, its paws cradling its jaw.

The boy stared at it. Sitting there, its shoulders hunched over, the beast didn't look frightening at all. It didn't look scary.

It looked sad.

The boy's heart slowed as he watched the Wolf lumber up to standing and trudge back behind the Green Wall.

A smile stretched out on the boy's face. He'd done it. He'd beaten the Wolf.

"*You were lucky.*"

"It wasn't luck." The boy shook his head. "I fought him."

"*You didn't kill him.*"

"I scared him. That's even better."

He jumped around the clearing, beaming at the sun and the clouds and the lighthouse.

"I scared the Wolf. I scared the Wolf."

"Hoo." The owl flittered around the top of the light-house, joining the boy's celebration. "Hoo."

"I scared the Wooolllllfffff!" he howled at the Green Wall . . . then hushed as a noise pricked his ear.

"*All right,*" the bully said. "*I guess you're not a complete los—*"

"Shhhhh!"

The bully obeyed. The owl fluttered back to its perch on the lighthouse railing, staying quiet.

The boy turned his head in the direction of the noise, and his heartbeat sped up again—this time from hope. Was that laughter? And voices? Real laughter from another person?

"*Don't believe it,*" the bully said. "*No one's coming for you.*"

The boy frowned. Hope had disappointed him enough,

but this sounded like a conversation. And it was different from the voices he'd heard before.

When he heard the noises again, the boy drew up straight. It *was* laughter, carried on the wind. It was laughter and words. And with them came the sound of wood scraping on tiny rocks.

He glanced around but saw nothing that could make these noises. So where . . . ?

The noises were coming from the south side of the lighthouse. Maybe they were coming from the gorge.

The boy rushed through the trees to the edge of rock jutting out over the small beach, the owl swooping behind him. Two small boats, one with two boys in it and the other with just one, were approaching the shore. Two of the boys looked older than him, but the third could have been another 10–12.

Was this one of his memories, like his bedroom or the tree house? Maybe, but he didn't recognize the boys.

They came closer. And closer.

If they were just a memory, wouldn't they have disappeared by now?

The strangers pulled their boats up to the gravelly beach. The boy at the back of the two-seater—the 10–12-year-old, wearing red shorts and no shirt—jumped out, his

bare feet splashing in the water. He pushed the boats farther onto land.

"Good! That's good," an older boy with a white T-shirt
shouted. "Take this." He threw the end of a rope to the
boy with the red shorts. "Tie it over there."

Red Shorts did as he was told. Then the boy in the other
boat, wearing a green T-shirt and brown shorts, shouted,
"Get this one," and he also threw an end of rope. Red
Shorts secured that one too.

Green T and White T clambered out of their boats.
Green T pulled out a blue box with a white lid. A cooler!
White T retrieved three fishing rods.

This couldn't be just a memory. They were walking
on the beach, and the boy could hear the crunch of sand
beneath their feet. They were striding right up the shore
into the rocky gorge. They must be real. Other people.
Here. On his island!

The boy's heart pounded

Who were they? Were they looking for him? Maybe
they had seen his boat. Maybe they . . .

Maybe they had been sent by his parents. He glanced
at the owl, sitting in a tree. It ruffled its wings but didn't
fly closer.

The boy's heart pushed against his rib cage, every pulse

more excited than the last. Excited to meet them. Excited to talk to them. But also nervous that they might leave him alone again.

"Hi!" he shouted. He waved, but the strangers disappeared beneath the ledge of the cliff. He sprinted to the opposite edge of the crescent-shaped hole for a better look.

"Use this to pull up." White T grabbed the end of a long, thick root, hanging from the cliff like a rope, and threw it at Red Shorts.

Red Shorts took hold of it, scrunched up his nose, and said, "It's sticky."

"Stop being a wimp. Grab it and pull yourself up."

"You want me to go first, Nate?" Green T said to White T, stepping closer.

N-a-t-e, the boy mouthed. White T's name must be Nate.

"Yeah, Ricky. You go first so Kyle won't be a chicken."

And Green T was called Ricky, and Red Shorts, the other 10–12-year-old, was Kyle.

"I'm not a chicken." Kyle let go of the root and crossed his arms.

"Here, Ricky," Nate said as he grabbed the end of the root and threw it at him.

With grunts and heaves, Ricky pulled himself hand over hand up the root and onto the ledge.

"Now you," Nate said to Kyle, handing the fishing rods up to Ricky.

The boy waved, but Ricky kept watching Kyle until he'd shimmied up the root. Nate followed, hauling up the cooler attached to a rope over his shoulder.

"Let's go," Ricky said, leading the others toward the lighthouse.

The boy ran around the cliff, standing between the strangers and the trees. The owl swooped behind him as his heart leaped. Finally, friends. Finally, a *rescue*!

He stood up straight. "Hi."

Kyle turned toward him and smiled.

REVELATION

THE BOY STEPPED CLOSER TO THE STRANGERS.
"You're here! You're here! I've been by myself for so—"

"This place is awesome," Kyle said.

"Oh, here?" The boy followed Kyle's gaze past him and out to the ocean. "I guess. But it's—"

"Can we go in the lighthouse?" Kyle headed toward it.

"Yeah, but . . ." The boy pointed toward the other island. To where he wanted to go. "I really need to get ho—"

"No, Kyle." Nate placed the cooler on the ground and lifted the lid.

The boy was relieved, but Kyle stopped and turned back to the older boy. "Why not?"

"Because we're fishing."

Fishing? They hadn't come for him? The boy put his hands in his pocket, felt the piece of fabric.

"Hey," he said, "you're here to take me away, right?"

"They're not going to take you with them."

"Shhh!" The boy bent his head, hoping the strangers

didn't hear. "I mean, can you take me home or to that bigger island?"

"You're not going anywhere."

"Shut up," the boy said through clenched teeth.

He glanced at the strangers. Had they heard? He didn't want them to see him talking to himself. They could think he was weird and leave him here. Alone. Again.

"Fishing first, then we can do whatever you want," Nate said.

The boy smiled. They would take him. They would! "Okay." He nodded. "Fishing first."

He hoped fishing wouldn't take long.

Nate pulled a small red box out of the cooler and clicked its latch. Placing it on the ground, he picked out rolls of wire; some kind of shiny, fishy-looking things; and an even smaller cardboard box.

"Where are we going to fish? From the beach?" Kyle kicked a Doritos bag on the ground.

"Not from down there. It's too shallow, doofus." Ricky opened the cooler and grabbed a Coke can.

"You're the doofus."

"You're the doofus," Ricky imitated. He pulled the tab of the Coke. *Pshhhtt.*

"Hey, don't have those now. They're for after," said Nate.

"Who cares about after? I'm thirsty now." Ricky gulped from the can.

A drink sounded so good. The boy lifted his hand. "Can I have one?"

"I'm hungry," Kyle said. He flipped open the cooler lid. "I want a sandwich."

Sandwiches? The boy's stomach grumbled. "Can I have a sandwich? I haven't eaten since . . . well, yesterday."

Nate shut the lid again. "We're not eating now. Fishing first."

The boy frowned. Maybe the strangers didn't realize how long he'd been on this island. He wondered what kind of sandwiches they had. Turkey? Ham? Peanut butter? His mouth watered. "I just—"

"So where are we going to fish then?" Kyle interrupted.

The boy shut his mouth and shot an exasperated look at the owl. The strangers were rude. But they had brought the boats, so he had to be nice. The owl seemed to agree, cocking its head.

Nate pointed to the cliff on the north side of the lighthouse. "On the ledge out over the water. Wait till you see. It's the best spot for fishing."

Kyle peered in the direction Nate was pointing. "Better than the pier?"

Ricky laughed. "Way better than the pier."

"Hey, it's flat with rocks over there," Kyle said, continuing to look around. "Why didn't we pull the boats up there?"

"Was climbing the root really that hard?" Ricky laughed.

"I just mean—"

"There are too many rocks around the lighthouse, and the current is too strong," Nate said.

"Duh," Ricky said. "That's why there's a lighthouse."

Nate glared at him. "It's easier to get the boats on that little beach and climb up. Ricky, where are the rods?"

"I left them by the root," Ricky said.

"They won't do us any good over there." Nate shook his head.

"All right, all right. I'll get them," Ricky said. "Keep your pants on."

The boy slumped on the ground. What was taking so long? Couldn't they see he wanted to go?

"They don't like you."

"That's silly," the boy whispered. "They don't know me. How can they not like me?"

"They think you're weird. Only weird boys get lost on an island."

"I'm not weird."

"What's that noise?" said Kyle.

The boy shut his mouth.

"What noise?" Nate looked up from the red box.

"From over there." Kyle pointed at the Green Wall.

The boy spun toward the trees. Was it the Wolf? It must have come back. He didn't want it to hurt his rescuers.

He jumped up. "Don't go near there! There's a giant Wolf inside. It tried to eat me, but I scared it off."

"*They're not going to believe you scared a Wolf.*"

"But I did!" The boy clapped his hands over his mouth. He had said that too loud.

Ricky started laughing, and the boy hung his head.

"That's the duppies," Ricky said.

"Duppies?" Kyle's eyes grew wide. "You mean like ghosts?"

"That's why it's called Duppy Island," Ricky said. "The whole place is haunted."

The boy shook his head. "The Wolf's not a ghost. It's real."

But nobody paid attention to him.

"Hoo," the owl said, and the boy nodded. If he showed the strangers, maybe they'd take him home. "Look here." He waved for them to follow him. "Here's where I beat the Wolf. Right here." He pointed to the gashes in the sandy grass where the beast's claws had dug into the dirt. "See? And it did this to my leg and my shoulder." He showed them the scrapes, which had started to ache. "Then the Wolf ran off through there."

He stepped closer to the Green Wall, pointing in the direction he'd last seen the beast.

HIIIIIIISSSSSSS.

The boy stepped away again. "There's that thing too."

Kyle started walking toward him but stopped when Nate stood up.

"What did you do with the hooks, Ricky?"

Ricky rolled his eyes. "They're right there."

"No, they're not. I've been through everything. I told you to put them in the box."

"I did!" Ricky strode to the red box. He picked it up and dumped the contents onto the ground.

Nate threw his arms in the air. "Why'd you do that?"

"You can see everything better this way," Ricky said.

"It'll get all unorganized." Nate knelt by the pile of wires and lures. "I still don't see the hooks."

Ricky sighed. He knelt down too, spreading out the tackle.

"Where *are* the hooks?" Ricky ran his fingers through his hair.

"I asked you to do one thing. That's it." Nate shook his head.

"I got the food," Ricky said.

"We don't need food to fish. We need hooks!" Nate's voice was angry.

The boy kept quiet. He glanced at Kyle, who was also standing a few feet away, watching the older boys argue.

"We can't fish now," Nate said.

"Come on," Ricky said. "We can do something. Just put the lures on."

"We can't catch anything without a hook." Nate sounded exasperated. "The lure just lures. The fish aren't going to hold on to the line on their own."

Tendrils of hope swelled in the boy's chest. If they weren't going to fish, maybe they could eat. Then go to the other island.

"Keep wishing."

The boy pinched his thigh, trying to shut up the bully, but the pain just made him wince.

"We've got to go," Nate said.

Finally! The boy straightened. Did he have everything? The square of fabric? He checked his pocket. It was still there.

He smiled up at the owl, and his new friend stared back

at him. He'd miss the owl, but he'd be with his family soon.

He was ready.

"We can get the hooks and come back," Ricky said.

"Yeah, let's do that," Kyle said.

Nate looked at his watch. "We don't have time."

"Sure we do," Ricky said. "It's not late."

"Kyle and I have dinner." Nate glared at Ricky. "Mom wants us back. It was hard enough convincing her to let us come today. I can't believe you, Ricky. You really messed this up."

The boy tried to hide his smile. He didn't want the strangers to think he was happy about Ricky's mistake, but he didn't care about fishing. He'd been alone on this island long enough.

"Whatever," Ricky replied. "You could've got the hooks too."

"Okay. Okay!" Kyle ran between them. "We'll come another day. If we hurry up, we can at least get some fishing in on the pier."

Nate looked at his watch again. "Yeah, maybe. All right, let's pack up. And don't leave anything behind, Ricky."

Ricky shook his head, crushing his Coke can in his hand.

"What can I do?" the boy asked.

"*Don't bother*," the bully spat. "*You're wasting your time.*"

"Kyle, help me with the tackle box," Nate said.

"I can bring the rods," the boy said, ignoring the bully. He walked toward them, but Ricky picked up the rods first, tossing his smashed Coke can at the base of the light-house.

"I can get the cooler." The boy hoped he could eat a sandwich in the boat.

"*You can be as sweet as you want, but they still won't take you,*" the bully said.

"Yes, they will," the boy hissed.

Kyle put the last lure in the red box, and Nate shut the lid.

"Okay, let's go." He handed the red box to Kyle. "Put this in the cooler and bring it on the boat."

Kyle walked over to the boy. He lifted the cooler lid and placed the box beside a pile of foil squares. The sand-wiches. The boy's stomach groaned.

Kyle closed the lid and reached for the handle.

"I can get it," the boy said. "I want to help."

He reached down for the handle too, but Kyle lifted the cooler at the same time—and the handle went through the boy's hand.

NOTHING

THE BOY FROWNED AT THE HANDLE OF THE cooler. *That was weird,* he thought. *It must've slipped out of my fingers.* Kyle *had* pulled it up quickly.

Kyle walked toward the cliff, following Nate and Ricky.

The boy ran beside the strangers, trying to ignore what had happened. He told himself it was nothing, that his fingers had just slipped off the handle.

But a bad feeling had clamped onto his gut, and it was growing stronger.

The boy bit his lip. He would show his gut that nothing was wrong. He got into step with Kyle, swinging his arm in time with Kyle swinging the cooler. The boy reached down. Touched the plastic. Gripped the handle.

"Yes!" he whispered to his gut. "See? You're wrong."

Then Kyle tripped on a pebble, abruptly halting his stride and the swing of the cooler.

The handle slid through the boy's fingers again.

Anxiety filled his chest as he pinched his hand. Rubbed the skin. What was wrong with him?

"Hurry up." Nate was handing the rods over the cliff. Ricky must have already been on the beach. The boy had to jog to keep up.

"You go first, Kyle," Nate said as Kyle got closer. "I'll take the cooler."

"Okay." Kyle grabbed the root and swung his legs over the edge of the cliff.

"Can I go next?" the boy asked.

But Nate didn't answer. Just kept watching his brother.

"They're going to leave you."

The boy shook his head. "Hey." He stepped in front of Nate. "Can I go next?"

"Watch your step at the bottom," Nate said. "Some of the rocks are loose."

"They don't want you."

"So I can?" the boy asked.

"Okay," Kyle called up.

"You're going to be here forever."

The boy set his jaw against the bully's words. He reached out for Nate's T-shirt. "Are you talking to me or him?" He grasped at the material, but Nate shifted away.

"All right, I'm coming now." Nate stepped forward, almost forcing the boy over the cliff. He jumped aside just in time.

"Hey!"

Nate ignored him. He grabbed the root and made his way down to the small beach.

"Wait!" The boy waved his arms.

"Forever and ever."

"Shut up!" the boy shouted to the bully, no longer caring if the strangers heard him. "Wait for me," he called to them. "Wait!"

But they didn't wait. They didn't stop. They walked on toward their boats.

"Told you."

The boy's heart shuddered. "I'm coming," he shouted. "Don't leave!"

He gripped the root, reaching his leg out over the wall of rock. "Don't look down," he whispered to himself. Climbing down the cliff was going to be scarier than it looked. The edge protruded far over the concave wall, so the boy wouldn't be able to touch the rock with his feet.

"I can't get this one untied." Kyle's voice rose up from the beach.

"I'll do it," replied Nate. "Get in the boat with Ricky."

The boy tried to concentrate. All he had to do was step off the cliff and climb down the root. Just like it was a tree in the forest. A really skinny tree with no branches to perch on. Nate and Kyle and Ricky had done it; he could too.

"Man, did you have to pull this so tight?" Nate was still on the beach.

"Wait!" the boy said. "I'm coming!" He pushed off the cliff. Twisting the root around his foot so he wouldn't fall, he lowered himself slowly. His hand slipped. He stopped.

Once upon a time . . . He breathed . . . *Once upon a time, there was a boy who scaled mountains. . . .*

"Leave it, Nate," Ricky said. "We'll just take this boat. We'll get that one next time we come out."

"Someone might take it," Kyle said.

"Nah," Ricky replied. "No one else comes out here."

The boy glanced down. Nate was looking out at the ocean, at the other island, where the boy wanted to go. He tried to hurry.

"Okay," Nate continued, "we'll leave the boat. But if my dad complains, I'm blaming it on you, Ricky."

"You blame everything on me," Ricky said.

"Only because you deserve it."

The boy heard the crunch of footsteps in the gravel. No! They couldn't leave without him. They couldn't.

"Wait!"

"Too late."

The boy tried to move his foot farther down the root,

but it was caught. The thick rope tightened around his leg.

Scchhhuuucck.

He craned his neck to see what was making that noise on the beach below. Nate was pushing the boat through the dense sand and onto the water. Ricky and Kyle were already inside, and Nate jumped in behind them when the boat bobbed on the surface.

"Wait!" The boy let go with one hand and waved. "My foot's caught."

"They're not waiting."

The boy tugged harder to release it. But the more he pulled, the tighter the root held on.

"WAIT!" the boy screamed. "Don't leave me. Please don't leave me here!"

He ripped at the root with his fingers. Tore off pieces until it loosened and let him free. He jumped the rest of the way, landing on his hands and knees.

"I'm coming!" he shouted.

But the strangers paddled away. Away from the beach. Away from Duppy Island. Away from the boy.

His heart sank.

They had left him here. All alone. He'd thought they had come to rescue him, but they'd left. And didn't even say good-bye.

His chest tightened, panic rising into his throat. His chance to escape was gone.

But there was one boat on the beach! If he hurried, he could catch up to them. They had acted strangely to him on the shore, but the boy shoved that thought away. They'd have to help him if he got to their boat. Wouldn't they?

The idea of going on the water brought back the dread that soaked through the boy, but he ran to the boat. He pushed it toward the tide, but it wouldn't move far. The rope! Why hadn't he remembered that?

He glanced at the strangers. He could hear their laughter over the water, but they were getting farther and farther away with every second. He had to hurry.

The rope was too tight. The boy wrestled with it.

"Come on," he said. "Get loose."

It wouldn't budge. He jiggled and wiggled and jerked the rope, but the knot stayed tight. He hit and pried and pulled the knot. "Please," he whispered. And it moved. Just a little.

"Better go."

"I've almost got it." He wrestled and hoisted and heaved—and the knot slipped more.

"I'm getting it!"

"You're going to get it. Look."

"What?"

But suddenly he knew. He had felt something on his toes but had tried to ignore it. Now he looked down. The tide had swooshed in. It was up to his ankles.

He heard a rumble. A grumble. A ROAR!

It wasn't the Wolf; it was deeper and louder. The boy turned to the gaping entrance of the gorge, and his heart lurched.

A giant wave was hurtling toward him.

The boy let go of the knot. He ran for the root. His feet slipped on the gravelly sand, but he continued to run. He had to get out of the gorge—fast.

As the wave raced closer, drops of water clawed through the air to get at him. Finally he got to the cliff face and grabbed the bottom of the root. He pulled and pulled and pulled himself up as quickly as he could.

Another roar bellowed below him. He glanced back. The wave was close. Too close.

"Hurry!"

"I'm trying!"

"Hoo," the owl called, swooping above him. "Hoo."

The boy hoisted himself higher. He was almost to the top. He reached up for the edge of the cliff, but a piece of rock gave way. He flailed. He fell.

"NOOOOO!"

He caught the root again. His fingers grasped tightly.

The *ROAR* echoed around the gorge. The boy gulped in air as the wave washed over him.

He held his breath and held the root. He shut his eyes and tried to stay calm.

"Trust me. Jump!"

It was the angry voice again. When he opened his eyes, the boy was no longer in the gorge. He was standing on a silver ladder, the rocky cliff replaced by pink tiles. His heart crawled into his throat.

"JUMP!" The word shrieked through his mind.

He opened his eyes and exhaled. He was back in the gorge and the wave had receded. But it was already coming back.

He didn't have time to wonder about the memory, why it wouldn't leave him alone.

"Move!" he shouted, spurring himself up the root until he was over the top of the gorge and out of the wave's reach.

The strangers were far away now, only specks near the other island. There were no waves around their boat. For them the ocean was perfectly calm.

The boy watched them go, his fear ebbing as his sorrow settled back in.

"Told you they wouldn't take you. You wanna know why?"

The boy shook his head. The bully would only have something bad to say, and the boy had had enough of bad. The lighthouse, the Wolf, the water. None were good to him. None helped.

"Because you're nothing," the bully said, ignoring the boy. *"Nothing. Nothing. Nothing."*

Nothing . . .

This time the boy didn't feel pain or shame at the bully's words. Something nagged at him, a pinch in his brain that he was missing something—something horrible.

Nothing . . .

His gut curdled. He thought back to the handle of the cooler and the conversation he'd had with the strangers. They'd ignored him when he'd asked for a sandwich, ignored him when he'd said he'd carry the rods and the cooler. They hadn't talked to him at all.

The boy dropped to his knees.

"They couldn't hear me." His words were barely a whisper. "They couldn't see me."

He stared up at the sky. The sun hid behind a cloud, blanketing him in shadow.

"I'm not nothing," the boy murmured. "I'm a ghost."

MEMORY

GHOST.

The word tumbled around the boy's thoughts.

Could it be true? Was he really a ghost?

He pinched his arm. "Ow!" If he were a ghost, how could he hurt himself? How did he stub his toe, or hit his head, or get scratched by the Wolf?

He twisted to see the gash again. It was still there, or was it? It seemed to flicker on his skin.

"This is weird."

"You're weird if you believe any of this."

The boy barely listened. He rubbed his hand over and over, replaying how the handle of the cooler had slipped straight through it. How the strangers had ignored him. How the ocean had been calm for them but had charged when he went into the gorge.

"It doesn't make sense," he whispered. "I can't be a ghost if I—"

He broke out in a run. His feet took him as fast as they

could back to the lighthouse. How could he break the floor of the house, but he couldn't hold on to a handle? How could he make the desk into a boat, but he couldn't make people hear him?

Wind swirled around him as he ran, picking up dust that trailed like ribbons. The snake of fear curled tighter and tighter in his stomach.

He reached the door and hesitated for a moment, two, three. If the house was as he had left it, with a hole in the floor and the desk missing, then he'd really done all those things and there would be no way he could be a ghost. But if it wasn't . . .

"You won't open the door."

"I have to know."

"You know what you are. You're a lost boy who nobody wants."

"I'm not so sure."

"What do you mean, you're not so sure?"

"The boys from the boat. The handle. The water . . ."

"It's all in your head. Those strangers were rude and mean and—"

The boy flung open the door.

The room looked exactly the way it had the day he'd first

come here. The desk sat by the wall. The floor was smooth
and whole. And everything was covered in a sheet of dust.

"This isn't right." He stepped back, back, away from the
house, his heart clamoring in his chest. "I *broke* that floor.
I *took* that desk."

He shook his head. This couldn't be. This was wrong.
Very wrong.

He touched his head, his legs, his arms. They were all
there, right where they should be—and they were solid.
His hand didn't slice through them like it had on the
cooler, like a ghost's would.

But the room . . .

Had he imagined doing all those things?

The snake snapped taut in his stomach. Fear screamed
through the boy. Thunder rumbled in the sky.

He dropped into a heap on the ground. Lightning
clapped overhead and raindrops thwomped onto the gravelly sand around him.

He thought back to when he'd first woken up on the
beach. Was there any sign that he wasn't a real live boy?
He had scared the birds when he'd shouted, but when he
was frightened, they'd turned terrible. He had looked for
footprints in the sand, but everything was smooth.

And he'd been hungry and thirsty just like a living

boy—but only when he thought of food and water.

"Maybe I imagined it was all real," he told himself. "Maybe because I believed it, it seemed like it really happened. But when Kyle moved the cooler, I couldn't pretend anymore . . . my hand went straight through."

"Sounds about right. And shows you're even more brainless."

"How was I supposed to know?" the boy said, bitterness shoved between every word. "If you don't have anything useful to say, shut up."

The bully fell silent.

The boy wished he knew something, could remember something, anything that told him why he was here, alone, a ghost and no closer to having any answers. No more memories that didn't help him. He needed answers.

But now, he knew, he'd never get them.

Sadness permeated every inch of his being. All he had was nevers: He'd never see his family again. Never play with his brother. Never hug his mother. He had wished so hard for all those things—traveled so far to get them—and for what? He didn't have a home. All he had was this beautiful island, and it was filled with horrors. Horrors he'd have to live with forever.

Fear wrapped around him, squeezed tight.

Thunder boomed. Rain gushed from the sky. The ground trembled beneath the boy.

"No," he whimpered, wishing he still had the blanket. He had probably imagined that, too, but at least it had been some comfort.

Lightning carved gashes between the clouds overhead, and the boy curled up on the gravelly ground. He shoved his hands into his pockets and . . . his fingers closed over the piece of fabric.

He *had* found something else when he was on the beach. It hadn't helped him then, but now the boy pulled the piece of fabric out of his pocket. It wouldn't cover him like the blanket, but it was comforting all the same.

"Once upon a time, there was a boy who wanted to stop being afraid."

He moved to rub the piece of fabric across his lip, but its color caught his eye. Bluish-gray, just like the blanket. He hadn't noticed before how similar they were. And now that he looked closer, he could see the same vertical and horizontal lines that had been in the corner of the blanket. They weren't just similar—they were same.

This wasn't any piece of fabric. It was the corner of the

blanket. And it was in his pocket. Had been since he'd woken up on the beach!

The boy sat up, not caring that lightning flashed above him.

The blanket wasn't from a hotel. It must have been *his* blanket. Somehow it had found him on the island, but before that, he had the square. He kept the square in his pocket, so it was always close. But why . . . ?

The storm grew around him. Shielding himself as best he could, he gripped the square in his hand, staring at it with all his concentration. "Once upon a time, there was a boy who could remember."

Wind roiled past his face, churning the dust and sand. The air grew thicker and thicker, until it blocked out the lighthouse and the Green Wall and the sea. The boy was trapped in a cocoon of wind and dust.

"See? We'll put it right in this corner." The words were calm and light, out of place within the dust storm. But they comforted the boy. He knew that voice now.

"Mom."

The haze parted in front of him and his mother came into view. She was sitting at a table, light streaming in from the window behind. The boy sat next to her, younger, elbows propped on the tabletop. A blue blanket was spread out on the table in front of them.

His mother placed the tip of a red Sharpie on the material.

"E-T-H-A-N. Ethan. It's all yours."

Smiling, she pulled the blanket off the table and held it up so the younger boy could see his name, red lines drawn onto the corner. He grinned.

"That's my name," the boy whispered, watching his memory. "That's what the lines were on the corner of the blanket. *My* blanket."

"Thanks, Mom," the boy in the memory said, taking the blanket into his hands.

The dust began to settle between the boy and his mother, and he reached out to touch her. But she was gone.

"Noooo—"

"The pirate king drew his sword on the knight. 'You won't take me,' he said." The voice surrounded the boy in the swirling dust. Another voice he knew: his own.

He whipped around and saw the dust clear again, this time showing him and his brother kneeling together on a wooden floor. The blanket hung off the tops of two chairs, forming a tent above them.

A book lay open between them, and the boy saw himself hold up a paper-towel tube like a sword. Next to him,
Ollie said, "I'm not a knight. I'm a pirate too. See, I have
a pirate hat." He adjusted the brown woolen hat on his
head. It stuck out in the corners like ears and had strings
that hung down over his cheeks.

"Nice pirate hat," the boy in the memory said, and they
both broke into laughs.

Watching, the boy laughed too. But as quickly as the
memory came, the dust closed it away.

"More," the boy shouted, and the dust obeyed.

"Is that tight enough?" His mother's voice.

She was with his younger self on a patch of grass. The
blue blanket was draped over his shoulders, and the boy's
mother was tying the corners around his neck.

The younger boy shook his head. "Make it tighter."

"You sure?" she asked.

"Yeah."

And his mother did.

"You're the handsomest superhero ever," she said.

"I'm a knight," the boy corrected.

"Of course you are," his mother said.

"You remember the knight's motto?" Another voice

echoed over the scene, as though it came from a different room. This voice was deeper, his dad's, and the boy in the memory nodded enthusiastically.

"Yes, sir," he said. "The smaller something is, the more it needs protection."

"That's right."

The dust covered them and the boy looked for the next memory. This time it was him and his brother in his bed, the bed he'd seen in the lighthouse keeper's house. The blanket was spread over them and the boy was rubbing the corner on his lip. A new sound mingled with the din of the wind, an angry howl that sounded like the Wolf.

The boy stiffened. Was the Wolf close? Even though he had beaten it once, the boy didn't want to face it again.

But in his memory, he and his brother scrunched farther under the blanket. And the boy realized the growl wasn't from the Wolf here, but from the wolf that scared them at home.

The sand shifted again, showing the boy riding a purple bike, the blanket streaming out from his shoulders . . . and again, showing the boy brushing his teeth under a dome of blue, lifting the blanket to examine his teeth in the mirror . . . and again, showing the boy and his brother playing tug-of-war with the blanket, until it started to tear. . . .

The rapid memories played one after another in the swirling dust, until they stopped on an image of the boy's father standing in the shallow end of a pool. The boy could see his father clearly now. They had the same nose, the same curly hair. He stood tall and wide.

And his eyes were a bright, shining green.

FATHER

IN THE DUSTY MEMORY, THE BOY'S FATHER was surrounded by pink rectangular tiles. He beckoned to his son, who was holding tight to the metal rungs of the ladder in the deep end of the pool.

"It's too deep," the boy heard his own voice call out.

"Don't be a sissy," his father said. "The best way to learn anything is to jump into the deep end. Do it."

"But Dad—"

"I'll be right here."

"But—"

"Don't whine. Do as I tell you. Trust me. Jump!"

The boy watched as his past self hesitated.

"Jump! JUMP!"

Fear propelled him into the cold water.

He fell down,

down.

Down.

All the way down until his toes touched the bottom. He panicked. His arms flailed. His mouth opened.

Water rushed in where air was supposed to be.

He wriggled and slashed, trying to get back up—until he got tired. He floated. Limp.

He felt a tug. His back hit something hard and cold. A weight pressed down heavily on his chest. And he coughed, water surging from his lungs.

The dust shifted again, and the memory showed himself under a blanket—a blue blanket—with his brother, a flashlight their only light. "*Shhhh*," the boy whispered. "It's just the wolf, just the Big Bad Wolf." He held his hands against his brother's ears, blocking out his parents' shouts from the next room.

"He could have died, Bob."

"He was fine."

"No, he wasn't."

"All he had to do was push to the surface. You touch the bottom and push off. It's not difficult."

"He's a child. What do you expect?"

"He's a coward."

"He's scared."

"I was right there. Nothing was going to happen to him."

"It's not that, Bob. He's scared of disappointing you."

"I'm afraid," Ollie whispered.

"Don't be." The voice from the boy in the memory had

bite now, like his father's. "Don't ever be afraid. You'll be weak. Do you want to be a coward?"

It brought tears to Ollie's eyes, and he shuffled away from his brother.

Watching, the boy felt his brother's pain. "I didn't mean it, Ollie," he told the memory. "I'm sorry."

The picture dissolved into dust, and the boy was again looking at himself, now sobbing outside a window, watching his parents in the house. His father held the blanket over a trash can.

"He's too old to keep playing with this," his father said. "Look at it, it's filthy."

"He likes it. Who cares if he still plays with it?" his mother replied.

"I do. He's the joke of the neighborhood." His father dumped the blanket in the trash. "And we have to start weaning that hat away from Oliver too."

His old despair grew deep in the boy's chest as the dust shifted again. His mother was sitting on the edge of his bed and pressed something into his hand. A small square of blue fabric with faded red lines.

"You make your own courage," his mother said. Her face held a smile, but her eyes did not.

When that memory faded, the air grew dark. All

around the boy, the dust slowed, then settled. He frowned. It was still day, but it looked like night. Then he realized the sun wasn't the only thing that had gone away. The lighthouse and Green Wall had disappeared too. He was standing facing an inky ocean. A fat moon hung in the sky, casting a line of white from the horizon to the beach.

Voices drifted across the breeze from behind him, and the boy turned to them slowly. Chairs and tables dotted the sand. He was standing on an umbrella beach.

His heart lifted, but not too far. There was something familiar about this beach. Something he didn't like. It seemed harmless enough, inviting even, with its powdery sand and shielded loungers waiting to make visitors comfortable. Behind, golden light streamed out of windows from a ground-floor apartment.

The boy had played chess with Ollie on that lounger, eaten breakfast on that table, made a castle with that sand.

Shadows moved inside the apartment, a man and a woman. Their shouts raged out of the open doors.

The shouts got louder and the boy huddled behind a chair, rubbing the piece of fabric between his fingertips for comfort . . . just like he'd done, how many nights ago?

He glanced around. Yes, this memory was different.

He wasn't just watching what had happened—he was experiencing that night all over again.

"Don't put this on me," the boy's mother said. "You're the one who wants everything to be so perfect."

"Perfect? I'd settle for mediocre!" his father shouted.

"He's trying."

"That's not trying, Jillian. Open your eyes. You can't keep making excuses for him. When he's older and facing the world on his own, are you going to go around to every job interview and say, 'He's *tryyyyiiiiing*'?"

"Shut up."

"No, you need to hear this. You coddling him is not protecting him."

"You're pushing him too hard, Bob. He's just a kid."

"He's old enough to start figuring things out on his own."

"He's scared—"

"Scared? There's nothing to be scared of if he just trusts me."

"Why should he trust you?"

"Are you blaming me for the pool . . . ?"

The boy closed his eyes, covered his ears, and curled up tight. But he couldn't keep their words out.

"That wasn't my fault," his father continued. "It wasn't."

"He's just a boy."

"And I'm teaching him to be a man."

"We're on vacation, Bob. Let the boys have fun."

"Ethan can have fun when he's learned how to sail."

"That won't make him become a man."

"Yes, it will. I'm teaching him to face his fears. He can't give up just because he's scared. Oliver, too. They have to toughen up, stop being so weak. You've coddled Ethan too much. I won't let you do that to Oliver as well. I'll make them both into men."

The words washed over the boy, and his eyes snapped open. He stared at the small sailboat on the sand, the one his father had tried to get him to go on earlier. The one that had made the boy so scared, he'd sobbed and almost peed his pants. He had nearly drowned once. Never again.

His brother had cried too, watching from the beach, knowing he'd be next.

But now his brother was asleep. And his father wasn't going to leave them alone. Not until the boy showed him, proved he wasn't afraid.

He gazed out at the endless water that seemed so calm, but the boy knew what water could do.

Still, if it meant Ollie would be safe . . .

"Once upon a time . . . ," the boy whispered. "Once

upon a time, there was a boy who pleased his dad. . . ."

He ran to the boat, shoved it into the water, and climbed in. His father had shown him how to use it. He pulled the rope that made the sail slide up the mast. He pushed the rudder so the boat turned out to sea.

He ignored the shouts and screams rising inside him, warning him that this was a bad idea—a very bad idea.

He sailed. Out into the ocean.

The night breeze skimmed cool kisses across his cheek. He felt free, alive. He had turned away from his fears, just like his dad had said, and he was sailing. Just him and a tiny cup facing the whole big ocean.

His name drifted across the wind: "Ethan? Ethan?"

It was his mother; her sweet, protective voice. But he didn't need it now. He was doing what his father wanted.

He would show him.

"Ethan? Are you out here?"

He was. He was sailing into the blackness of the night, the velvet sea carrying him to become a man.

"Ethan!"

Sailing away from his fears and weaknesses.

"ETHAN!"

Sailing away from his insecurity and pain.

Until— "NOOOOO!" his mother screamed.

"Bob!" she shouted. "The boat is gone. He took the boat out."

The words swam over to the boy, and he smiled.

"I'm doing it, Mom!" he shouted back. "I'm sailing!"

But a gust of wind slapped his words back into his mouth. He tried to shout again. But his words were whisked away.

Both his mother and father were shouting and running toward the water now. His father's voice was edged with anger and worry. "Ethan! Come here right now! Ethan! Come back!"

Yes, he could go home now. He had shown them. He had sailed.

The boy pushed the rudder to turn the boat back toward the shore—but it was heavy. Above him, the sail was fat with wind, quickly carrying him away from the beach, away from his parents.

He tried to cry for help.

He tried to shout.

He tried to scream.

But his words were lost in the churn around him.

The wind blew stronger and stronger. The boat twisted in the water like it was being spun by a giant invisible hand. Round and round and round.

Water rose up beneath him. And the tiny cup was carried away.

Waves rocked the boat from every direction. Splashed over the side and onto him. Tearing at his arms and legs. Pulling him toward the edge. Trying to drag him under.

He struggled to keep the water out, but big waves came from opposite sides, crashing into the boat. The bow rose. The boy tried to hold on, gripping the sides with all his might.

But it breached, crashed down, breaking in half. The mast tipped over. Smashed the rudder. Cracked onto the boy's head.

He drifted . . .

    down,

        down,

            down into the water.

Back on the cliff, the boy opened his eyes and gasped for air. It was day again and the lighthouse towered over him, shimmering through his tears.

"I'm dead," the boy whispered. "I'm dead."

Knowledge is the bridge between Belief and Truth.
The boy didn't have the whole picture,
but he understood enough.
When he put together the final piece,
his fear would rise up again.
It would take over, like in so many poor young souls.
Hope wouldn't change the boy's path—
or what I had to do.
The time had come. My wait was over.

I let the boy see me. . . .

CHOICE

THE BOY STRAIGHTENED AS I APPROACHED. He had gained more courage in his time here, but I knew it wouldn't last. His biggest challenge was yet to come.

I stepped toward him cautiously. His eyes crinkled. His heart sank. His mind filled with the new information he thought to be true: *I'm dead. I'm a ghost. He won't see me, just like the strangers.*

"Hello, Ethan," I said.

His eyebrows rose as he sat up. "You're talking to me?" His voice was small and broken.

"Yes, Ethan." I nodded.

"You . . ." He paused, pointed his finger at me with an arm too apprehensive to be extended all the way. His mind was trying to decide who I was, how I came to be here, how I knew him. "You can see me? You know my name?"

I nodded again. "I know a lot about you. I've been waiting for you."

"Waiting for *me*? I've been here for ages. You're the one who just showed up."

I paused. This was the difficult part. Adults accepted it quicker than children. I had to handle it carefully.

"I've been here too. I've been watching you."

I felt his anger rise; he didn't try to suppress it. He let it overflow into his chest, then out of his mouth, a tide that had been held back since the moment he had woken up on that beach. I understood. I expected it.

"What do you mean, watching me? I haven't seen you." He scrambled to his feet. He wasn't finished, so I let him continue. He needed the release. "Why didn't you tell me?"

"You didn't know what had happened to you, Ethan. I had to wait until you knew, until you remembered."

Tears welled in his eyes, but he blinked them back hard. It wasn't just me he was angry with. I learned that early in this job. His outburst carried with it all the abandonment he felt, all the confusion, hurt, and disappointment that had built up in his short life. Once the dam is cracked, the feelings tumble out.

"I remember everything." His voice was sour. "I know who I am, and I know what happened. That horrible water took it all from me." He glared at the ocean beside us, then back at me. "You should've said something. You should've told me."

I didn't reply. He didn't need to know how my job worked. *I* had to know about *him*.

Waves crashed against the cliffs around the lighthouse, higher, higher, as the snake of fear twisted in the boy's stomach. He balled his hands into fists.

"The water ruined everything," the boy said. "I had to do something very important. I had to help someone very important!"

He fell silent, just the waves disturbing the sound of his thoughts. It is easier for the elderly. They let go quickly after they remember, when they have the full knowledge of what's happened to them. Whether they felt it was their time or not, most are happy to turn away from the uncertainties of life, and then my service seems noble. For the young, it is much harder, on me and for them. They have so much more to lose—a life not yet lived—and yet they still let fear take it from them so often. I do not understand why.

The boy was still holding on to his past, gripping it tightly as though it might get away. But I knew he'd let go eventually, like so many before him.

"What did you have to do?" I prodded. He had to fully let go before I could collect.

"*Don't trust him,*" the bully said. The boy glanced at me to see if I'd heard. "*He doesn't care about you. He's just like your dad. If he cared, he'd have helped you earlier. He'd have told you the truth."*

The boy narrowed his eyes. "Who are you?"

"I am a Spirit Collector. I'm here to—"

"For spirits." The boy spat out the words as though they didn't taste good in his mouth. "So you know what I am."

I nodded.

"And you know what brought me here, about the sea." He glared at it again.

I nodded once more. His anger was building, so many emotions in so small a soul.

"You should've warned me!" he said. "If I'd known I'd end up here, like this, I'd never have gone on the stupid water. I wish I'd never . . ."

The rest of the sentence stung his mind. He wished he'd never sailed the boat. He wished he'd never gotten in the accident. But there was a bigger wish, the more terrifying wish: that he hadn't *needed* to go . . . to be a man for his father . . . to help his brother.

His brother's small face filled the boy's thoughts, and sorrow ripped through him.

"Now my brother's alone without me," he said. "He won't be able to be perfect. He'll get scared because I'm not there to help him. . . ."

There was more he wanted to say; fear, hurt, and worry built inside him. But the bully took over.

"You're too weak."

"I'm too weak."

"You're too cowardly."

"I'm too cowardly."

"You're a wuss."

"I'm—"

The boy collapsed on the ground, despair growing with every sob. I put my hand on his shoulder. He flinched, but he didn't pull away. He needed me—or at least, some other being. They all do, whether they want to believe it or not. Once the anger subsides, they all want to be comforted.

"I'm dead," he said. "I failed. I'm dead and there's nothing I can do."

"Actually," I said, "there is something you have to—"

"Hmmmmm mmm mmm mmmm." The tune blossomed around us, waltzing in the air. It was his mother's voice, and the boy knew her immediately.

"Mom!" The pain rocketed back into his head and he clamped his hands around it.

"Hmmmm mmm mmm mmmm," she hummed.

The boy released his head, pushing through the hurt,

and gazed into the sky. Searching. Wishing. Hoping.

"Come on, Ethan," she said. "Come home."

Her words were bright and warm, like the light that had brought him here, to the place where he had found the map and his answers.

"Mom." His brain throbbed, but he reached his arms up and brought her words down to him, hugging them against his chest.

"It's time to come home," she said. "It's time to wake up."

The boy's eyes lit up, his tears forgotten, as his face twisted into a confused frown. "She's telling me to wake up and come home."

"Spirits, or souls, can hear the voices of their loved ones," I said, "but—"

"Wake up, Ethan. Wake up."

The boy's eyes sparkled for this voice too. "Ollie!" he shouted to the air, then turned back to me, realization growing. "They want me to wake up. I thought this was a memory, but it's not, is it? They're talking to me."

I confirmed with a nod.

"If they want me to wake up, I must not be dead. Right? But . . . How . . . ?"

"I've been trying to tell you—"

"I *didn't* die in the accident. I'm alive!" He screamed the words to the sky, to the clouds, to the bully.

His attention returned to the pain in his head, and he brought his hand to it like he had when he first woke up on the beach.

"I was only hurt in the accident," he said.

"You were hurt very badly. You suffered a lot of injuries. And—"

"But I'm still alive."

I paused. He was being persistent. That wasn't unusual. Many before him had held on to their hope a long while, until it was eclipsed by fear. He needed to accept, then he could move on.

"Your heart is still beating," I said.

He put his hand over where his heart would be, if he were in his body. He could feel it, even though it wasn't there. It always amazes me how they keep their heartbeat going even as spirits. It's an old friend. They do not want to be without it.

The boy nodded slowly. He was trying to understand.

"So my spirit is here and my body is . . . Where am I? At home?"

"Your body is in a coma in a hospital on the other island.

It's sleeping, but it can't go on much longer without you."
I tried for a reassuring smile. "I'm here to collect you. I'll
help you to move on."

"Good." He stepped closer, the pain in his head dissipating once more. "Take me home now."

I frowned. It's awkward to have to explain this too
much.

The boy misunderstood my pause. "Please?" he added.

My lips pressed together, a gesture I'd learned from the
thousands of spirits I've faced over the years. I shook my
head.

"I can't take you home."

"Why?" His anger was back, growing within him like
a volcano.

"I am here to help you move on," I said, emphasizing
the last word. "You make the choice, then we go."

"Yes, I'm making the choice. I want to go back." He
thought of Ollie again, and his anger simmered into anxiety. "I *have* to go back."

I shook my head. "If you want to go back, you have to
make that choice. And *you* have to take the action."

He crossed his arms. He sensed what I meant but didn't
want it to be true. "What do you mean?"

"If you want to go back to your body, you have to go there." I pointed to the island. "Yourself."

His arms dropped to his side. His stiff jaw slackened. He turned toward the hump on the horizon, the long stretch of ocean, and shook his head.

Fear. It falters everyone.

BULLY

THE BOY'S MIND WAS ABLAZE WITH thoughts, bad thoughts, terrifying thoughts. And the bully wasn't helping.

"It's out there. It's waiting. It's going to finish you off."

"I have to get past it," the boy said.

"You can't. You're not strong enough."

"I have to try."

"You won't. You're a chicken. Coward, wuss, sissy, wimp . . ."

The boy slumped under the weight of the bully's words.

"It's not nice to hear that, is it?" I asked.

The boy's eyes grew wide as he faced me.

"You can hear . . ."

I smiled. A lot of comfort can be found in a smile. "Yes. I can."

His eyes fell. The bully was silent now, but I knew it was still there, pouting.

The boy shook his head. "I don't like hearing it."

"Why do you listen?"

He looked at me as though I'd asked him why the sun

rises every day. "It's always there. It's hard *not* to listen."

I nodded. Thoughts can be difficult to ignore.

He walked away from me a few steps, to be alone. Shame and sadness swam around him.

Finally he turned back. "What will happen if I don't go home?"

And there it was, the question I had dreaded hearing yet had known would come since the boy first tumbled onto the beach. The question every spirit asks when they're about to give up on life.

"A spirit has only two choices: go back to your body and live—if that's possible, which in your case it is—or move on and your body will die."

"I know that." The boy stared at me as though I were dense. It took me aback.

"I mean, what will happen to my brother?" he continued. "What will happen to Ollie?"

"I can't answer that."

He crossed his arms tightly over his chest. "Can't or won't?"

I suppressed a laugh. The boy had surprised me; that didn't happen often.

"People make their own choices," I told him. "I can't know what your brother's future will bring."

I stared at the boy, so small in this big world. So unsure of what he was, or what he could be. He uncrossed his arms, dug his toes into the sand.

"You know what will happen."

"I know what will happen," the boy whispered.

"But it's too bad for Ollie, because you won't do anything about it. You can't."

The memory of his brother loomed in the boy's mind. Ollie's button nose. His little mouth. His scared eyes sticking out from under his brown woolen hat that made him look so much like a small baby owl. The boy had told his brother he'd help him, then told him not to be a coward. Just like his father. Just like his father would continue to do.

Deep in his heart, the boy felt he hadn't helped Ollie then—hadn't but should have.

A slight doubt wormed into my prediction of how the boy's story would end. I watched and waited as the thought that he hadn't done everything he could for his brother grew bigger and bigger, until it took over his mind.

He stuck his hand in his pocket and pulled out the blue square. He rubbed it between his fingertips.

"I helped the crab," he said. His voice started small but

got progressively louder. "I protected the owl. I fought the Wolf."

"That's nothing compared to what's under that water."

"Not nothing." The boy straightened. "I did that. What have you ever done, other than say bad things about me? Huh? What?"

The bully didn't answer.

"I've come all this way, found the lighthouse, got the map, everything," the boy continued. He turned to me. "If I don't go home, I'm going to die anyway, right?"

I nodded, a hopeful smile budding within me. He understood well.

The boy set his jaw. "I made a promise to Ollie. If I'm going to die, at least I'll do it trying to help my brother."

"NO! You can't do this!"

The boy strode to the edge of the cliff. He had determination, and my hope for him swelled. But I'd been disappointed before. I'd seen young souls try only to be taken by fear.

As he stared at the vast gap of water between him and his body, the boy's heart beat faster, and with it rose the waves. He faltered.

"See? This is ridiculous. Go back to the lighthouse."

"I can't swim across," the boy said.

"*Of course you can't!*"

"But . . ."

"*No. No buts.*"

"There's a boat. A real one this time."

"Hoo." The owl flew out from where it had been watching on the lighthouse railing. It circled over the boy, hooting.

The boy ran back through the thin crop of trees south of the lighthouse, toward the gorge. He peered over the side and there it was: the boat the strangers had left behind.

I followed, keeping my distance. I admired that the boy was still holding on. But his fear had already begun to curl and twist within him. Dark clouds raced across the sky. Wind howled off the surface of the ocean. Waves crawled up the gravel beach.

"*There's no way you'll make it home.*"

The boy rapped his knuckles on his head. "If you leave me alone, I might."

"*The only way I'll stop is if you're never afraid again, and that's not going to happen.*"

"Why can't you believe in me?"

"*Believe in you? Why should I? You always give up. Always! Sure, you got the blanket, but only after it drifted to the shore. And sure you escaped the Wolf, but only because it walked away. And remember the boat you made? You did all that work, then your sissiness just let it go. You haven't figured out anything. Why should I believe in you?"*

The boy gulped back his emotions, then whispered, "Because I need you to."

There was a pause. Then, in a low voice, the bully said, "*Show me you deserve it.*"

"No," the boy said, shielding his face from the sand blowing around him. "We do this together."

"*What am I supposed to do?*"

The boy looked up at the owl, bobbing and swooping in the windy air. "Say I can do it," he said.

"*But—*"

"Say it!"

"*Okay. Fine. You win (although you probably won't): You . . . can . . . do . . . it. Happy?*"

The boy stared out at the sea. The waves rolled larger, and high above, lightning ripped open the sky.

"It's a start," the boy whispered.

He grabbed the root the strangers had used and swung himself over the edge.

MONSTER

WIND TORE AT HIS BODY AND HIS HEART pounded in his chest. He had barely gone down two feet when he heard the giant *ROAR* behind him. The wave slammed against the boy before he had a chance to hold his breath. He gripped the root as tightly as he could while the water pushed and tugged and wrenched at him, before retreating back out of the gorge.

Shivering, the boy scrambled back up to the cliff, his chest heaving, his breath heavy.

Another wave crashed in the gorge, higher and harder than the last one. When it retreated, the boy knew it would be back, stronger than before.

Thunder *CRACKED* above. Lightning streaked behind the trees. The next wave came with a *ROAR*.

Then another . . .

Then another . . .

Then another . . .

The boy shook his head. Put his hands over his ears.

"Stop," he whispered. "Please, stop." The water was

going to ruin everything again. It was going to break the strangers' boat. Destroy his last chance of getting home.

The boy watched the owl, struggling and bracing against the rippled air. He thought of his brother, of the *ROAR* of the Big Bad Wolf.

"Once upon a time . . . there was a boy who braved the storm."

He took a deep breath, calmed his heart, and shouted, "STOP!"

The lightning retreated, pulling away the clouds. The sun shone down on the boy again, and he smiled.

"Hoo," said the owl, flittering above his head.

"Whoa," said the boy, eyes wide.

"*How did that happen?*" said the bully, sounding a little amazed.

The boy peeked into the gorge. The boat was exactly where it had been left, tied up on the sand. The rest of the beach looked normal, as though giant waves hadn't just swept through it.

"That's why everything always got better when I was safe. The storms come when I'm scared, right?" He turned to me for confirmation.

I gave him a smile. My hope for this boy was rising—hope that I wouldn't have to collect another young soul. But he wasn't home yet, and I had seen too many others give up.

"Our fear is what we make of it," I told him.

The boy nodded. But I could feel in his heart that he knew it wasn't this simple. He still had to get across.

"Hoo," the owl said, as it settled on my shoulder. The boy smiled at it, a thin smile filled with all his hope and doubt, fear and courage.

Then he turned away. He grabbed the root, flung himself over the side, and shimmied down quickly before his fear rose again. At the bottom, he ran to the boat and tugged on the rope. It was tight, but the boy pulled harder and the knot unraveled. "Yes!"

The boy secured the paddle, then pushed the boat to the water's edge. It was calm, but I could already see his imagination at work, churning the sea farther out.

"Once upon a time, there was a boy who could sail," he said.

He jumped into the boat and picked up the paddle, pushing it through the water as hard as he could. Back and forth. Back and forth. Pushing far, far away from the island. Far from the Green Wall, the beach, and the little home that wasn't his.

He felt his fear, but he jammed it down as far as he could, into the tips of his toes, where it couldn't bother him anymore.

"I'm doing it," he whispered to himself.

He looked back, just a peek. The island was now in the distance, the lighthouse a luminous monolith rising from the cliff.

"I'm doing it. I can do it! I'm going home."

He thought of his mother, her face smiling at him.

He thought of his brother, his eyes bright and shining.

And he thought of his father—the good part of his father, cheering when the boy rode his first bike, putting a Superman Band-Aid over a cut on the boy's knee, and kissing the boy on the head . . . just because.

The boy would be with them all soon. And he would show them. He would show his father. He'd prove that he could be brave.

No, he wouldn't show his father. He'd show *himself*. He was going to prove that he wasn't a failure. Even if he had to keep trying.

He pulled the paddle harder, back and forth, back and forth. Switching sides to keep his course straight. Straight out to the other island. Straight out to his home.

The sky was pink now, the sun preparing for bed. Long ribbons of rosy clouds drifted over the island ahead. And they were reflected in the shiny water, making the whole ocean blush around him.

A piece of a memory wormed out of the cabinet he had locked it in. Tiles. Pink rectangular tiles. The water below him. The water around him. The water pulling him down . . .

The sky darkened above. A harsh wind blew up and snatched the paddle out of the boy's hands. It dropped into the water, floating away.

"No!"

The boy reached over the edge of the boat to get it. But the water bit at his finger.

He froze. The hairs on his neck stood up. And all his fears rushed back into his heart.

"You didn't think this through, did you?"

"I—"

"Too late now. You're in the middle of the ocean. Miles and miles and miles of water all around you. And you have no paddle."

"I just—"

The surface of the sea pulsed around him. Ripples

surrounded the boat, pushed up by . . .

    something deep underneath.

        Something big.

            Something that was coming . . .

The wind picked up, clawing at his face and body.

The boat began to rock, harder and harder.

The boy trembled, his hands holding tight onto the sides.

With a giant *RRRROOOOOOOAAAAAAAARRRRRRR*, the ocean in front of the boy rose up.

An enormous spiraling cone of water lifted into the sky and grabbed hold of the dark clouds above. Big as a mountain, blocking out the sun.

Beneath the boy's boat, the ocean swelled. Balls of hail pounded onto the surface and the boat. Waves snatched at the sides, trying to get inside.

The boy's heart pounded. "Don't be scared. Don't be scared."

He glanced up, but the wall of water grew thicker. "Once upon a time, there was a boy who . . ."

Threads of water lashed out of the cone and hit the boat. The boy crouched down small, his arms over his head, and closed his eyes. "Once upon a time, there was a boy who . . ."

The cone spun across the surface, churning the ocean around him.

"It's not working. I can't stop it."

Another loud *ROOOOOOOAAAAAAAARRRRR* exploded beside the boy, and he trembled. Two more cones of water swirled out of the surface and attacked the blackened clouds. They looked like giant tentacles, writhing up from the ocean into the sky. The closer they got to the boat, the more the ocean bucked.

The boy curled himself tighter, smaller, but he couldn't get small enough. His hands shook as they tried to protect him. His heart shuddered in his chest. His whole body begged for the sea to stop.

The bully's voice penetrated his fear. *"You're in your own worst nightmare now. And you can't get away. See? I told you. You're brainless. And weak. And scared."*

"I know." The boy's words came on a broken breath.

"The water's going to get you. It's going to drag you down. Down. Down to nothing."

"I know."

"And it's all your fault."

"I know." The boy gulped back his sadness. "I'm sorry, Ollie. I can't get home. I'm sorry."

I sighed.

I prepared to collect his soul.

JUMP

THE BOY COWERED IN THE BOAT. I DIDN'T need him to row back to the island, but I did need him to make the choice—to let go. I was about to tell him, when I heard three words:

"Don't give up."

The pain bloomed in the boy's temple again, but it was lighter than before. He squinted against it—and stared into the glowing green eyes of the Big Bad Wolf. The beast sat hunched over on the other side of the small boat.

"You can do this, Ethan." It was his father's voice. Thicker, gruffer, but the boy still knew it was his father.

"The monsters are too big," the boy said, glancing at the tentacles of water thrashing around his boat. "I can't beat them all."

"You can come back to us. I know you can."

Muscled waves flexed under the boat, driving it up, then crashing it down.

"AAAAAAHHHH!" the boy screamed, crouching lower and burying his head in his hands. "I can't!"

"You can do anything you want to do."

The boy didn't move; he didn't look up. His shoulders sagged with the weight of his worry. He broke into sobs, as the world thrashed around him.

"I'm sorry, Ethan."

The boy stopped crying. He lifted his head and stared at the Wolf. The hair around its ears was graying, and its green eyes glowed with love and sorrow.

"Forgive me," the Wolf said. "I shouldn't have pushed you so hard."

"You wanted me to be brave," the boy said, sniffling away his tears.

"I thought that by pushing you I could make you stronger, but I was wrong."

The boy frowned. "What do you mean?"

"You're already strong," the Wolf said. "In your head and in your heart." The beast tapped a curved claw against his head, then his chest.

The boy didn't answer. He didn't know how to respond.

The tentacles pummeled the surface. Waves crashed against the side of the boat as it tumbled in the rocky ocean.

"It wasn't you who was afraid," the Wolf continued. "It was me. I didn't want you to become like me."

The boy sat up, holding on to the sides of the boat.

"What do you mean?"

"I was always afraid when I was a child," the Wolf said. "And now, I'm still afraid. Afraid I'm not strong enough, I'm not providing enough . . . I'm not enough. I thought that if I pushed you harder, you'd be different. But I was wrong. You can do it on your own."

"I'm not so sure," the boy said.

Screeches and roars emanated from the water. Louder and louder as the tentacles flailed.

"You are more than enough, Ethan. All by yourself. The way you help your brother . . ." The beast smiled, sharp yellowed teeth glinting out of the side of its mouth. "You are much stronger than me."

"Ollie." The boy thought of his brother. Would he be all right if the boy didn't make it home? Would the Wolf help him now?

"Ollie needs you, Ethan. He misses you. Your mother misses you. I miss you. We love you very much. We need you to come home."

Tears sprang to the boy's eyes again. "I want to come home, Dad. I love you, too."

He stood but was knocked back down. The whirling tentacles were so close now, the boy could feel their wind whipping against his face. Water had collected in the bottom of the boat and swirled around his feet.

"We're going to sink!"

The boat tipped wildly. Rocked back and forth.

"What do I do?"

"You know the way home, Ethan," the Wolf said.

The boy frowned. "I do?"

The Wolf nodded. "You know the way home."

Another giant wave crashed over the boat. It tilted dangerously. The boy held on.

"I know what to do. I know what to do," he muttered, trying to think of what he should do.

Then he remembered the pink tiles. The pool. The water. If he jumped, he'd be able to float. He'd roll over the waves and maybe—hopefully—make it home. It was risky. The ocean was much bigger than the pool and the water much more rough. But the boat wouldn't last long in this storm. He had no other choice.

He had to believe.

He had to try.

"On three, we'll jump," he told the Wolf.

"What? This is your worst idea yet. The absolute worst!"

"No, it's not," the boy said.

"You think you're brave just because ol' green eyes over there says you are? You're not brave. You're not strong. You're nothing. Nothing. NOTHING!!!"

The boy stomped his foot. The boat swayed in protest, but the boy didn't curl up. He didn't hide. He widened his stance so the boat was more stable.

"You want to know what the worst idea I ever had was?" He punched the air as he shouted.

"What?"

"Listening to you. You're the one who's brainless. Not me!"

"I'm brainless? You're the one in this boat. In front of that monster. Don't you get it yet? You're going to get yourself killed! You're going to get US KILLED!"

The boy's breath caught. "You're scared."

"Huh?"

"That's what it is. You're scared of us failing and getting hurt, so you *want* me to give up."

The bully stayed quiet.

"But if I don't do anything, the monsters will never go away!" The boy pointed up at the swirling tentacles, each as wide as a house and closing in on the little boat.

The boy pulled back his shoulders. "Of course I'm scared. But it's not about being scared. It's what you *do* when you're scared. I have to do this, and you're just gonna have to trust me."

"*I...* "But the bully fell silent. When it finally spoke, its voice was small. *"All right. Let's do this. But if you're wrong, I reserve the right to say I told you so."*

The boy grimaced. "If I'm wrong, you won't have to."

A deafening cry came from the ocean. The tops of the tentacles had converged right over the boat. They were colliding—on top of him.

"You know the way home, Ethan," the Wolf said.

"Yeah, you know."

The boy nodded.

The bases of the tentacles swirled closer, closer, closer, then crashed over the boat. As the hull splintered into a million pieces, the boy screamed, "JUUUUUUUUUMP!"

And he jumped.

A splash.

A gasp.

Then silence.

The boy held his breath.

Opened his eyes.

Darkness.

His heart tapped. Tapped. Tapped.

A small smile, then his arms pushed down. He kicked his feet.

He floated.

The boy bobbed on the surface of the ocean.

The giant tentacles were gone. The boat was gone. The beast was gone. The boy was alone, in the middle of the ocean.

"It'll be all right," he told himself. "Once upon a time, there was a boy . . ." He smiled slyly. "A boy who made his own courage."

He heard voices in the distance, quiet and warm. And he saw the light coming for him.

The beam shone out from the lighthouse, stretching across the rugged sea until it touched the boy's head.

He reached up his arm and disappeared.

HOME

I STOOD WITH THE BOY AT HIS BEDSIDE, listening to his imaginary heart beating wildly. No spirit finds it easy to look at his own body, lying lifeless, often covered with tubes. That's how the boy's body was, one arm in a cast, his head wrapped in a bandage, and I could feel the sadness within him.

But it wasn't sadness for himself.

The boy stared at his father, slumped over his son's feet. One arm was stretched up onto the bed, his hand clasped around his son's fingers.

"You know the way home, Ethan," the man whispered, his green eyes staring at his son's face. "You know the way home."

I can't see into the hearts of the living, but I didn't need to see in this man's heart to know his feelings. And neither did the boy.

In a chair behind her husband sat the boy's mother, her head leaning back, her eyes closed, music rising from deep within her heart, "*Hmm mmm mmmm. Hmm mmm mmmm . . .*" Her arms circled the boy's sleeping brother on her lap, a brown woolen cap pulled tight over his head with corners that stuck out as though he were an owl.

The boy's gaze washed over them but returned to his father, confusion, worry, and love tangled up inside him.

"You faced your fear," I said, smiling down at the boy. "Your father would've been proud."

"He won't know, will he?" the boy asked.

I shook my head. "You most likely won't remember yourself."

"I'll know," the boy said. "I'll feel it."

He turned to me. "I didn't mean what I said before, when I got mad at you for not warning me."

"You were scared." I gave him a small shrug. "I understood."

"Yeah, but I don't want to get mad when I get scared anymore. It doesn't help." He looked back at his father.

I wanted to ask him more, how he held on to his hope, what made him believe, what drove his courage, but he turned back to me with a wide grin and my questions were no longer important.

"I think I'm ready," he said, "but I'm still a bit scared."

"That's all right," I said. "You wouldn't be human if you weren't scared."

Watching his father's face, he understood that now.

"Okay," he said, standing taller than he had that first day on the beach. "What do I do?"

"Just close your eyes and want to wake up."

The boy closed his eyes, scrunched up his forehead in concentration, then opened his eyes and looked at me again.

"Hey, what made that hissing noise in the trees? I didn't like that."

I smiled. "Iguanas. Perfectly harmless."

"Oh."

He gazed at his toes, and when he lifted his eyes back up to meet mine, they brought with them a crooked smile.

"Thank you," he said.

He turned back to his family. And he was gone.

I stayed in the hospital room for a while longer and watched as the boy opened his eyes. I could no longer hear his thoughts, as I had from the moment he had washed up on that beach, but I could see the fear on his face as he tried to recognize where he was and why the tubes were lying across him.

I beamed at him, this small, small boy with a big heart and even bigger courage. I had been wrong about his story. Maybe you can't tell the strength of a person until you've seen inside their fears. Maybe a person can't tell their own strength until they can face their doubts.

The boy . . . *this* boy had created his own happy ending. I hoped it would continue—until the next time I saw him. He gave me hope that more young souls would fight for a life no matter how much they feared. He gave me hope that I wouldn't have to collect them.

He let out a groan, and his father stirred, head rising up, alert. He stood and leaned over his son.

"Ethan," he said. He brushed the boy's hair away from his forehead. "I'm here, Ethan. You're okay. You're going to be okay."

"Dad."

The boy's voice was quiet. His father leaned closer.

"Yes, Ethan, it's me. It's Dad. I'm here."

"Me too, Dad. I'm here too."

His father's smile grew so big, it barely fit his face.

The boy closed his eyes again, and his father frowned. He moved closer to his son's ear. "I'm sorry, Ethan," he said. "I'm so sorry."

"Dad?" the boy whispered.

"Yes, Ethan." The father's hands enveloped his son's.

"I jumped. For me. I jumped." And the boy smiled.

The father looked confused but patted his son's hand. "You did great, Ethan. You did great."

The boy's mother opened her eyes, then shook the younger boy awake. They stood, small screams of delight escaping their lips.

"Ethan." The mother filled the boy's name with wonder as she stared at her once-lost son.

"I'll get the doctor," the father told his wife. "I'll be right back, Ethan. Mom and Ollie are here."

As the father left the room, the younger boy ran to the bed, reached up, and grabbed his brother's hand, their fingers intertwining.

The boy looked from his brother's eyes, so like his own, to his mother's, so loving.

"Mom," he said, "I'm hungry."

It was less than a minute before the boy's father led doctors and nurses back into the room. Worry and hope were still etched on the father's face as he picked up the younger boy and embraced the mother. But as tears streamed down their cheeks, they all looked happy.

Their son was home.

I stepped back and smiled. My job was done. I had another spirit to collect.

I hoped her story had a happy ending.

Acknowledgments

You would not be reading this book if it weren't for the kindness, encouragement, and support of so many people. First, my husband, Jamie, who hasn't stopped saying this story is special since he first heard the kernel of the idea and helped me brainstorm more. Thank you for putting up with my middle-of-the-night writing sessions, for talking me through plot points, and for always believing in me, even when I can't. My parents, Paul and Fay Anne de Freitas, who have listened to my stories since I began writing plays for puppets when I was six. Thank you for showing me the world and all the stories it has within it. My college professor, Rick Wilber, who told me I had important writing ahead of me. I hope I'm living up to that. And God, who gives me strength and lifts me up both in my writing and life.

A huge thank you to Bethany Hegedus, who "got"

this story early on and has been an amazing friend and mentor to me and my writing. To Kathi Appelt who chose this book to win her year-long mentorship for the Houston SCBWI Joan Lowery Nixon Award—as well as for her continued encouragement and friendship. And to this book's first critiquers in the Houston SCBWI Clear Lake Critique Group, including Grey McCallister, Sara Joiner, Kimberly Garcia, Mary Ann Hellinghausen, and Laura Rackham; my early Austin critique group including Sheryl Witschorke; and my beta readers over many, many drafts, including Donna Janell Bowman, Meredith Davis, Holly Green, Vanessa Lee, Salima Alikhan, Shelli Cornelison, Nikki Loftin and any I've missed. My words are better thanks to you.

An enormous thank you to Donna for pitching this book to agent Liza Pulitzer Voges, to Liza for recommending it to agent Rachel Orr, and to Rachel for her unwavering championing of this novel and all my work. To my editor, Sarah Jane Abbott, for her love of this boy and his world and her brilliant help to make the story better. To Sylvie Frank and Paula Wiseman at Paula Wiseman Books for their warmth, enthusiasm and support. To everyone at Simon & Schuster who welcomed me into their family of authors and have worked so hard to make this book beautiful and connect it to readers, including Ellen Grafton, Chava Wolin, Valerie Shea, Vanessa DeJesus, Anthony Parisi, Sarah Woodruff, the wonderful marketing, sales, and foreign rights teams, and especially to Laurent Linn who I'm lucky to have as a friend and an art director. And to Justin Hernandez who put so much passion into his amazing artwork for this book.

And thank you to the VCFA College of Fine Arts literary magazine *Hunger Mountain*, which published an excerpt of this book, back when it was called *WAKE*. To SCBWI and all the staffers and volunteers who give so much to children's book writers and illustrators around the world. To my wonderful Austin SCBWI family, including Cynthia Leitich Smith for always having time for advice and a kind word, and to my incredible fellow Lodge of Death writers for being a constant inspiration. To the amazing authors who generously gave their time to read and blurb this novel, you are the greatest! And to all the librarians, book reviewers, readers and, of course, YOU for opening your hearts to stories like mine—thank you.

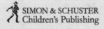